NAGUIB MAHFOUZ
Heart of the Night

NAGUIB MAHFOUZ
Heart of the Night

A NOVEL

Translated by Aida A. Bamia

The American University in Cairo Press
Cairo   New York

This edition published in 2020 by
The American University in Cairo Press
113 Sharia Kasr el Aini, Cairo, Egypt
One Rockefeller Plaza, New York, NY 10020
www.aucpress.com

Dar el Kutub No. 26766/19
ISBN 978 977 416 998 4

Dar el Kutub Cataloging-in-Publication Data

Mahfouz, Naguib
        Heart of the Night / Naguib Mahfouz.—Cairo: The American University in Cairo
    Press, 2020
        p.   cm.
        ISBN 978 977 416 998 4
        1. Arabic Fiction—Translation into English
        2. English Fiction—Translation from Arabic
        892.73

1 2 3 4 5   24 23 22 21 20

Printed in Egypt

1

I looked at him closely and said, "I remember you very well."
He bent over my desk, his foggy sight fixed on me. His proximity,
his roaming look, and his efforts to see clearly, revealed his weak
eyesight. Seeming unaware of his closeness to me and the small size
of the quiet room, he said in a harsh, high-pitched tone, "You do! I
do not trust my memory anymore, and on top of that I do not see
very well."

"The days of Khan Jaafar cannot be forgotten!" I said.

"Welcome. You are from that district then?"

I introduced myself and invited him to sit down. He said, "We do
not belong to the same generation but there are things impossible to
forget." He sat down. "I believe I changed completely. Time has
placed on my face an ugly mask of its own making, not the one my
father gave me."

He proudly introduced himself, though he did not need to. "Al-
Rawi. I am Jaafar al-Rawi, Jaafar Ibrahim Sayyid al-Rawi."

I was not blind to the pride he felt in saying his full name. There was
a strong contradiction between his miserable look and his proud tone.
He continued to reminisce.

"You take me back to some very dear memories, to the blessed district
of Khan Jaafar and al-Hussein, the days of happiness and adventures."

"There were some exciting incidents and strange stories," I said,
provoking his laughter. His tall, thin body shook so much, I worried his
worn-out suit might tear.

He raised his tanned face toward me, scratched his head covered
with gray sticky hair, and said, "We are family, and I am entitled to be
optimistic about the fairness of my case."

1

I asked him if he wanted a cup of coffee, to delay possible disagreements. He replied boldly and without hesitation, "Let's begin with a fuul sandwich, then order me coffee."

I watched him eat voraciously, and was filled with sadness. His smell stayed with me, a mixture of sweat, tobacco, and mud. After he ate and drank he sat up and said, "Thank you. I do not want to take up any more of your time. You must have seen my request by virtue of your position. What do you think?"

I said regretfully, "No use. The waqf system does not allow such a thing."

"But the truth is as clear as the sun."

"The waqf is also clear," I said.

"I studied law, but it seems that everything changes."

"Everything except the waqf. To this day it has not changed."

He roared in his rough voice: "My rights will not be lost! Let the Ministry of Awqaf know that." Then, seeing my calm smile, he grew quiet and asked to meet the director.

I said gently, "The matter is very clear. The al-Rawi waqf is the largest in the Ministry of Religious Affairs. Its proceeds are held in trust for the benefit of the two holy mosques and the Imam al-Hussein mosque, in addition to charitable organizations, schools, monasteries, and public fountains. A charitable waqf cannot, by any means, be owned by anyone."

He interrupted me, explaining his position: "But I am the grandson of al-Rawi, his only heir, and in urgent need of a penny, whereas the Imam al-Hussein is happily settled in paradise."

"But it is a waqf," I repeated.

"I will take legal action."

"It will be useless."

"I will consult a sharia lawyer, but it has to be free of charge, because money is an unknown entity in my world."

"I have many friends among the sharia lawyers and I can arrange a meeting for you with one of them, but do not waste your time running after a hope that will not materialize."

"You treat me like a child."

"God forbid," I said. "I am only reminding you of a reality that you cannot change."

He went on, "But I am al-Rawi's grandson. This is easy to prove."

"Yes, but al-Rawi's estate became a charitable waqf."

"Is it fair that I should be left to beg?"

"The procedure for a person in your situation is to submit a request asking for a monthly donation from the waqf income, on condition that you prove your relation to the owner of the waqf."

"A monthly donation," he repeated. "How unfair! How much would that be?"

I hesitated for a moment. "It might reach five pounds or slightly more."

He laughed sarcastically, revealing black, broken teeth. "I will fight, you'd better believe it! I have lived a life that even the jinn would not put up with. Let the battle commence! I will not stop fighting until I obtain my rights in full from the inheritance of my wicked grandfather."

I could not help smiling. "May his soul rest in peace and reward him for all the good he did."

He thumped my desk with his fist and said, "There is nothing good about a man who forgets his grandson."

"Why did he forget you?" I asked.

He clutched his chin but did not answer. I felt that the storm would clear sooner rather than later, and that he would end up writing a request for help like the many other descendants of pashas, princes, and kings in our country. I was convinced that no one rejected his heirs for no reason. What had you done, Jaafar?

He turned his failing eyesight toward the empty space and went on, saying, "Establishing a charitable waqf, and depriving me of the inheritance, that was how he always conducted himself, combining bad and good. He continues to exercise his power now that he's dead, as he did when he was alive. And here I am, struggling after his death as I did during his lifetime, and will continue to do until my death."

3

2

My relationship with Jaafar al-Rawi grew stronger with time. In his loneliness, he was ready to cling to anyone who would encourage him, be it only with a smile. I ventured into this friendship with the strong conviction that it would end soon. His disturbed personality did not suggest a desire to settle down into a lasting friendship and it did not take much to satisfy him. There were obvious reasons that drew me to him, but there was also an intangible motive: past memories and my own fascination with the al-Rawi family, their stories, the rumors about Jaafar's crazy adventures, and my attraction to Jaafar despite his repulsive appearance. I felt sorry for him, living his final days in this miserable way. He was quite tall, and were it not for his poverty and possibly some illnesses, his old age would have been glorious and beautiful.

One day, after a meal of kawari in one of the Muhammad Ali Street restaurants, I asked him how he lived. His answer was quick. "I roam the streets during the day until almost midnight."

"Where do you live?" I asked.

"Among the ruins."

Surprised, I asked what ruins he was referring to.

"They belong to me by reason of occupancy. This is what is left of my grandfather's house."

I did not know that the house had fallen into ruin, as I had not visited the neighborhood in a very long time.

"Don't you have relatives?" I asked.

"They might fill the globe."

I smiled.

He explained, "I have children who are judges and others who are criminals."

"Is that true?" I asked.

"And despite that, I am alone."

"What a way to talk!"

4

"Give me back the waqf and I promise you that I will be surrounded by children and grandchildren. Otherwise I will remain alone, an outcast."

"You seem to like puzzles," I commented.

He laughed. "I like a good meal and the waqf. I'd also like to damn those responsible for the waqf."

"Don't you have any income in your old age?" I asked.

"I have some old friends. Whenever I meet one of them, he shakes my hand and puts in it whatever he feels like giving me. I roll in the mud now, but I originally fell from the sky."

Saddened, I said, "This is not a way to live. Write your petition immediately."

"It is the true, authentic life. Try it if you have the courage. Open doors boldly, don't be servile: everything you want is your right. This life belongs to the human being, to everyone. You have to get rid of your stupid habits; that is all you need to do."

"Yet you wish to regain your grandfather's inheritance," I said.

Laughing loudly, he said, "Do not hold me responsible for my contradictions. I am a pack of contradictions. Don't forget also that I am an old man, and have been engaged in a battle with my grandfather for a very long time."

"I'd like to know why he deprived you of your inheritance."

"This is my battle," he explained. "Do not rush matters. I am not the simpleton I appear to be. Many are fooled by my appearance, and young children even follow me as I roam the streets. Do they think that I like to talk? Because I am alone, I talk to myself. What do people think? I am getting older, and I have not stopped asking questions. Believe me when I tell you that I am not a normal person. Even when I was on the mountain or living in the palace or in the ruins, I was not normal. Despite my loafing and begging, I stand tall in life, my head raised high and defiant, because life respects only those who do not take it seriously."

I smiled as I watched him defying existence, wearing his worn-out suit and with his tanned skin. I whispered, "Good for you."

5

He went on, talking about his connections. "I do not interact with humans alone, but I have contacts with non-human things: jinns and devils and the intrinsic components of civilization." He then changed his tone and asked, "Have you chosen a trustworthy lawyer for me?"

I pleaded with him, "In God's name, Jaafar, forget this imaginary case."

"Am I not Jaafar Ibrahim, the grandson of Sayyid al-Rawi?"

"You are," I said, "but you do not have a case, none whatsoever."

"I will provoke a revolution that will reverse the order of the universe."

"That is more feasible than winning your case. Write the petition and do not lose time."

Laughing, he said, "The employees of the waqf ministry live off the income of our properties, then they stretch out their hands to offer us charity."

"Write the petition and do not lose time."

Silence fell over us for a few minutes, and then he said, as if talking to himself,

"Five pounds!"

"You must at least rent a room on a roof."

"No. The amount will be enough for food, cigarettes, and clothes. As for lodging, how can I rent a room when I own a palace! I will not leave the ruins."

I told him once more, "Write the petition as soon as possible and send it to the ministry."

"There's no rush. Let me think about it. I might write the petition or I might consult a lawyer. I might even go on with my life without a petition or a lawyer. No need to rush."

"You know what you should do," I said.

"There is no possibility of communication between the two of us. You fear life and I despise it. What you fear even in your imagination I have endured, and everything you ask God to spare you I have sought with my own free will."

"This is great, Jaafar," I said.

"Do you like what I say?" he asked.

"Very much."

"Would you like to hear more?"

"I assure you that I would."

"You have treated me to a wonderful meal and will offer me serious help in the coming days. We are the children of the same neighborhood, so let's go to Wadud's café at the Green Gate."

We walked side by side in the direction of the old neighborhood, passing beneath the historic arch that leads to the Green Gate. There we settled down, smoked hash, and drank coffee, and talked in the quiet of the long night.

3

Bab al-Akhdar alley fell into silence under cover of night. It is then that the hordes of beggars return to their spots, the lunatics clutter the corners, and the smell of incense fills the air. No outsider roams there at night except the few customers of Café Wadud. They are all hash smokers.

"Let me tell you about the time of the legend," said Jaafar.

"You mean your childhood years," I said.

He was quick to respond, "I mean what I said, so do not interrupt me. There is no childhood, but a dream and a legend, the age of the dream and of the legend. It forces itself on you in a tender and possibly deceitful manner, usually because of the hardships of the present. It echoes strongly in my psyche, but when I analyze it I come out empty-handed, which confirms its illusionary nature. Suffice it to say that I know nothing of any significance about its two basic poles, my father and my mother."

"Did they pass away during your childhood?" I asked.

"I do not remember my father at all, and I have no visual memory of him. He did not leave a photo to remind me of him. He left the world before fathering another child. I remember only one incident connected to him, and that somewhat obscurely. It was on the day of the celebration of the mahmal, as we watched from a window overlooking Margush. I was sitting on his shoulders watching the crowds and the head of the golden mahmal swaying at the level of the window. It was a situation imbued with compassion and affection, don't you agree? The mahmal is one of the landmarks of the legend. As for the crowds, they were a special kind of reality. The memory revived one day in my office in Bab al-Khalq square, making me shout in Saad Kabir's face these words—"

But I interrupted him, "We are in the midst of the legend. Do not overstep its boundaries!"

"Let me talk freely. I hate restrictions."

"But the story will be scattered by the stream of thoughts and I might lose my way between its fragments."

He laughed loudly. "Won't you allow me to toy with time the way it toyed with me? Well, let's go back to the legend, to the brazen jinn, to the playful inanimate objects, to the spectral truths, and to the real dreams. I have already told you that I do not remember my father, but I will never forget my mother's hand."

"Your mother's hand?"

"Be patient," he said. "My father died, but I do not know how or why. He died in his youth, as I was told years later. I was five years old or slightly younger, and unable to even remember the house in Margush district. There was possibly a room that could be accessed from the hallway via two steps. There was also a high bed that could be reached by climbing on a wooden stool that was very tempting to play with, and a water pipe was placed high on top of an armoire, out of my reach. There were spoiled cats, a mangle, a dark storeroom inhabited by all types of jinn, black mice, an incense holder, and a clay jug seated on a tray, filled with water in which sliced limes floated. There were also a coal heater and sacks of coal, chickens, and a conceited rooster. I do not know what caused my father's death or what his job was, but I can tell you about death itself. I am an expert in it. I once deserved the title of life giver because when anger takes over and words turn to flames, swallowing the celestial words, mysterious doors open, through which devils slip. Satan himself arrives in his fiery parade, surrounded by judges, policemen, and jailers. At that moment Jaafar al-Rawi changes his name, his surname, and his skin."

"But what about your father's death?" I asked.

"May God forgive you," he said. "You crush inspiration. You insist on learning how my father died as if he were your father. What do I know about his death? I woke up on a dark night to discover that I was in my mother's arms and she was taking me to the neighbor's. I must have fallen asleep, and when I awoke in the morning I found myself in a strange place. I cried. When the neighbor brought me food, I asked her about my mother. She explained, 'Your mother is running an errand and will be back soon. Eat your food.'

"I ate despite my anxiety, as I was continuously hearing crying; though in a way, crying and ululations were a usual thing in our neighborhood. I went back home that night, or the following day, and found a strange and gloomy atmosphere. I felt there was a painful secret that I could not decipher, but one that made me feel weird and anxious. My mother had changed completely. She was dressed in black, her face was pale, and she looked sick. Her gaze had withered and seemed worn out. The house had lost its wholesome atmosphere and genuine cheerfulness. I asked her, 'What is wrong with you, Mother?'

"'Everything is fine. Play,' she said.

"'Where is my father?'

"She turned her face away from mine and said, 'He is on a trip. Go on playing; you have the whole roof. Do not ask so many questions.'

"Her attitude toward me had changed: she was rough and unconcerned. My mother was avoiding me; she was avoiding my gaze and my company. She cried behind my back. My father did not return from his travels. I was not totally ignorant. I had heard things about God, the devil and the jinn, paradise and hell. I had even heard threatening things about death that had nothing to do with joy. I was wondering when my father would come back and when my mother's face would return to its usual serenity. My anxious wait for my father lasted a long time. I was overcome with despair about his absence, but when precisely I lost hope in his return and how I forgot him and went on with my life as if nothing had happened, I can't remember. There is no way I can recall all that, but I will never forget my mother's hand."

"You have mentioned your mother's hand many times already," I said.

"She would hold my hand or I would hold hers, and we would wander together in the alleys and souks."

"To shop or for pleasure?" I asked.

I was getting used to his live soul among the ruins and the memories. He seemed happy and grateful for the dinner, and for the hash he smoked, and for having an attentive listener for his story.

He said, "Sometimes I try to remember my mother's image but I can't see it. How tall was she? I was naturally much smaller than her and always looked up whenever I spoke to her, but this in no way indicates anything or measures her height. I have no idea about her weight either, or the color of her eyes or skin. I have a rather vague idea of subdued tones and movements. I remember strong emotions, smiles and laughter, and reprimands that were closer to visions from dreams. I can, however, affirm that she was beautiful, and had it not been for her beauty the tragedy would not have happened. I remember a comment made by our neighbor on a forgotten occasion: 'Hey, Jaafar, son of the beautiful woman!' But she did not live long enough to give me time to protect her image from destruction. Only the memory of her hand has stayed with me. To this day I feel her touch, her pressure and her tugging, and when she let go, as we walked from one place to the other across covered and uncovered alleys, among hordes of men and women, donkeys and carts, in front of shops and saints' tombs and monasteries. She took me to the gatherings of the lunatics and the fortune tellers, the sweet vendors, and the toy sellers. On those trips, I wore a gallabiya and a colorful hat decorated with an amulet.

"My mother's conversations were varied and contained a poetic tone that she adopted while talking with all creatures, each in its own language. She would address God Almighty, the prophets and the angels, and the holy men in their tombs. She even talked to the jinn, the

10

birds, inanimate beings, and the dead. She would interrupt her conversations with moans about her bad luck. The world around us was alive, aware of those conversations that it received and returned and participated in through its hidden will in our daily life, without discrimination between an angel and the door of a saint's tomb, between the hoopoe and the gates of old Cairo. Even the jinn mellowed to her magic words and this saved me from numerous dangers."

Noticing his serious demeanor, I could not help but laugh. Surprised, he asked, "Why do you laugh?"

I said apologetically, "You are narrating a dream that you can now interpret and explain."

He replied, "Do not think you know the world half as well as I know it."

"Is that so?"

"I am a sea of knowledge and I say that without boasting."

"But you do not differentiate between truth and fiction."

He explained, "There is no 'truth and fiction,' but different kinds of truths that vary depending on the phases of life and the quality of the system that helps us become aware of them. Legends are truths like the truths of nature, mathematics, and history. Each one has its spiritual system. Let me give you an example. One day my mother took me to visit my father's tomb, located in an open area among the tombs of the poor. She addressed him, saying, 'Your wife and son greet you and ask God to have mercy on you, most beloved and generous person. I complain to you about my loneliness and my misery. Pray God for us, oh beloved.' I then stuck my ear to the wall of the tomb and heard moaning and words that I repeated to my mother. She told me, 'You are blessed to the Day of Judgment.'"

"What did your father tell you?" I asked.

He replied, "You are not qualified to believe me and therefore I won't tell you."

I had a feeling he was covering up his playfulness with an appearance of harsh seriousness, or that he wanted to surround his legend with an appropriate atmosphere to satisfy his heart's nostalgia.

11

I mumbled, "For every learned man there is someone more learned than him."

"Our world was alive, throbbing with desires, feelings, and dreams. It was a mixture of seriousness and joking, joy and sadness; and all—humans, jinn, animals, and inanimate objects—equally shared in relationships of understanding."

"But do you understand all that?" I asked.

"Completely, passionately, and doggedly."

"Weren't you overcome with fear?"

"Sometimes, but I soon acquired tools of defense and attack and became the master of the world. One evening I was playing with the lemons spread around the water jugs on the windowsill, when I suddenly saw the head of a being level with the window, looking at me from the street. His eyes were alight in the dark and his legs were planted in the ground. I was troubled and moved away, falling on my back. My scream ripped the silence of the night. I later learned that the encounter between a human and a jinn should not take place in this manner. My mother told me that it was high time I memorized the Samadiya. As for the jinn of our house, those that lived in the storeroom, they were inclined to joking and were incapable of any serious harm. They were in the habit of mixing cheese with honey or hiding the clarified butter for their own use. Sometimes they extinguished the light of the lamp carried by people at night. Their worst jokes, however, consisted of changing dreams into nightmares."

"Can you give me an id ea about how they looked?" I asked.

"No, you are not predisposed to believe," he said. "Moreover, the jinn disappear from a person's life at the end of the time of the legend. He quickly forgets them and even denies their existence, though he encounters them daily in new images of human beings. In such situations they commit serious evil and cause great harm. You insist that the jinn are a mere superstition. On the other hand, I had the good luck of seeing the holy light on Laylat al-Qadr, the night of destiny, while sitting on my mother's lap looking at the sky! A window opened and out of it came a bright light that dimmed the light of the stars."

I laughed and told him, "It is said that only those who are destined for a life of happiness see the light on Laylat al-Qadr."

He laughed as well. "Touché! You beat me this time, but only to an extent. It is true that I am the example of extreme wretchedness, but what counts is how all this will end. The end is still unknown and I might find the answer in paradise. I happen to have a long history with paradise. My mother used to talk to me about it as if she had been there. I fell deeply in love with it, my mind spellbound by its vision. It became my fascinating dream, the magical paradise where one could see, hear, and talk to God, a garden with rivers, music, and eternal youth.

"But let's go back to my mother's conversation and how she managed to live after my father's death. I asked myself this question but could not answer it. We used to leave our house every day, visit the saints' tombs and the shops, buy whatever we needed, and then return home, where my mother busied herself with housework, while I went to my earthly paradise, among the cats and the chickens. Sometimes our neighbor visited us. I did not have relatives and neither did my mother. To this day, I have not found out if she had money. She dressed in black after my father's death and cried whenever she was alone. I often discovered her crying. And finally I understood the relationship between her crying and my father's disappearance.

"'Don't you say that my father is in God's hands?' I asked her. She nodded approvingly. 'Why do you cry then?' I asked.

"'I know it is wrong to cry, Jaafar, but tears flow despite myself.'

"This did not discourage me from pursuing my daily adventures. I would proceed joyfully, collecting eggs, chasing mice, and defying the jinn. My adventures lasted for a whole year after my father's death, and then I became attracted to the stories told at the sound of the rabab in the coffeehouse located under my window. I listened to them with great interest, as much as I could understand them, and I saw fights break out between the supporters of the different heroes of the legends. From the same window I watched bullies fight in weddings, and my admiration for them equaled my admiration for the jinn. I dreamed long of becoming a bully in case I failed to become a jinn."

"Have any of your childhood dreams been fulfilled?" I asked.

"Do not make fun of me, and be patient. I want to talk to you about love in the time of the legend."

"But the time of the legend is not the time of love!"

"I experienced love at age six," he said. "I liked to sit in the midst of girls during Ramadan nights. The only serious beating my mother gave me was because of love, when I had seduced a girl my age and took her to a wooden box and pulled down the cover. No sooner had I settled down than I was surprised by someone removing the cover. When I looked up, I saw my mother's shocked look and felt her braid touch my face. By the way, it was a very long braid and I used to play with it whenever I could. I would undo it, tie it, and twist it like a rope. My mother was undoubtedly beautiful, and, as I have already told you, were it not for her beauty, the tragedy would not have happened in the first place."

"Tell me about childhood love," I said.

He laughed. "It seemed like an aimless pastime, but I do remember that it was filled with sharp reactions. It was almost like being drunk."

"This is abnormal!"

"I am not a moralist, but I can assure you that sex was not an overpowering factor in my life. It played a decisive role during a specific time only. During my childhood, however, it contributed in its own limited way to the creation of the legend, but the legend received an unexpected and fatal blow. One day I woke up alone without my mother's help, and I became aware of that when I saw her deeply asleep, lying face down. I was happy to have the opportunity to wake her up for the first time. I placed my mouth close to her ear and called her name a few times, but to no avail. She did not respond. I shook her gently, calling her at the same time. Gradually my voice rose and I shook her more strongly, but received no response. I went on stubbornly trying to wake her up, my voice filling the room. I was desperate, and ended up leaving the room.

I took a pomegranate from a dish and went up on the roof. Peeling the fruit, I ate its amber seeds and gave the bitter part to the chickens.

"I saw our neighbor. We talked, and the conversation turned to my mother and the way I had left her in her room. The neighbor questioned me carefully and finally asked me to open the apartment door for her. She rushed to my mother's room, bent down, and then struck her breast with her hand, shouting, 'What a calamity! Oh Umm Jaafar!' She came to me, lifted me, and held me against her chest. Then she took me to her house. Her behavior saddened and oppressed me, reminding me of similar behavior when my father had disappeared for good. I cried, saying, 'I want my mother, I want my mother.' I spent two miserable days in our neighbor's house. They were the worst days in the time of the legend. At the end of the second day the neighbor calmed me down and said, 'Do not worry, Jaafar, God is merciful and compassionate.'

"I said, desperate, 'I understand, my mother went to be with my father.'

"Her eyes filled with tears and she whispered words of encouragment. 'God is with you. He is the father and the mother. He is everything.'

"Her husband intervened, saying, 'Something must be done, even if it means going to the government.'

"His wife replied, 'Even a stone would feel sorry for him.'

"Days passed while I lived absentmindedly, lost in my thoughts, until the neighbor announced cheerfully, 'Rejoice, my dear, God is merciful. You will be going to your grandfather.'

"I did not understand anything she said. I was hearing the word 'grandfather' for the first time."

4

Surprised, I asked him, "For the first time?"

"Yes, for the first time."

I asked again, "He was never mentioned during your mother's lifetime?"

"Never, though he lived in the same neighborhood."

"Why did she keep you in the dark about him?"

"Maybe because she was upset with him. Anyhow, our neighbor explained the relationship to me and told me that he was my father's father. His house was not too far from Margush, and in a way it was a familiar place, as my mother and I often walked by its high walls on our way to al-Hussein.

"I remember that I once asked my mother about the wall that stretched up quite high, like a mountain in front of the vaulted roof of the judge's house. She explained briefly and hastily, saying, 'It is a prison where criminals spend their lives in darkness.'

"The wall was not isolated from the other houses, in keeping with the tradition of design in popular neighborhoods, where the houses of the poor and the rich are adjacent. Nothing could be seen of the house or its garden. The only thing visible was the wall, which overlooked the treasury. It was a stone wall, long and high, truly like a prison wall or the wall of a citadel, and its door opened onto a dead end.

"I saw the garden for the first time when we crossed the gate. I had no knowledge of gardens, had not even seen a plant, except for a palm tree in the square where the judge's house was located and a cactus tree in the cemetery. My ears filled with the singing of a nightingale and the chirping of other birds. The branches were filled with those multicolored birds flitting around. I saw a flock of pigeons hover over a tower behind a vine-covered trellis. The tower overlooked a creek that crossed the garden from one side to the other. A gardener holding a basket in his hand was standing in the middle of the garden, his legs sunk into the ground up to his calves. I was overwhelmed to the point of intoxication by the mixture of heavenly scents that invaded my nose. Mesmerized, I could hardly contain myself from expressing my enchantment at the top of my voice. I walked down a path bordered by colorful flowers, on my way to the salamlik.

"The neighbor squeezed my hand and whispered in my ear, 'Jaafar, this is your new home.'

"I was totally bewildered. I saw my grandfather in the middle of the salamlik, sitting on a sofa with arabesque designs carved into its high back. My neighbor had a short talk with my grandfather, kissed his hand, then left. I found myself alone with my grandfather, not yet recovered from the magic of the birds, the flowers, and the stream; and the profound sorrow in my heart had not subsided. My grandfather sat cross-legged, wearing a large white robe and wrapped in an embroidered shawl, his head covered with a white cap. He had a long, thin face, brown skin, a large forehead, and a long, proud nose. His look was peaceful, and his white beard reached his upper chest. We exchanged a glance, and I did not see anything frightening on his part. He appeared quite old to me, but had a noble and distinguished demeanor. He looked like a worthy owner of that fascinating garden.

"I stood at some distance from him, neither close nor far. I was wearing my striped robe and my embroidered cap with the talisman attached to it, and colorful slippers. I carried a package containing my few belongings. He looked at me for so long that I was overcome with the urge to run away. Then, as if he had guessed my reaction, he smiled and directed me to come closer. I told him eagerly, 'I want to go back to my mother.' He held out his hand, and I walked to him and shook it. I was suffused with an urge to cry, but I controlled myself and did not shed a tear. His touch filled me with warmth.

"He said gently, 'Welcome,'" and sat me beside him. 'You are in your house. Do you like the garden?'

"I nodded eagerly to express my admiration, but he asked me to speak up. 'Talk. I like words.'

"I mumbled an inaudible 'Yes.'

"My grandfather asked me if I knew who he was and what being a grandfather meant.

"'My father's father,' I said.

"'Do you believe it?' he asked.

"'I do.'

"He asked if I remembered my father.

"'He used to carry me to see the mahmal,' I explained, 'but I remember my mother.' I then broke into tears, but he tapped me on the back and asked if I remembered something else about my father.

"'I visited his tomb,' I said.

"He turned his face away from me, then asked, 'What is your name?'

"'Jaafar.'

"'Jaafar what?'

"'Jaafar Ibrahim.'

"'Jaafar Ibrahim Sayyid al-Rawi. Repeat after me.'

"I did as he asked, and he went on questioning me. 'Who created you?'

"'God.'

"'Who is your prophet?'

"'Prophet Muhammad.'

"'Do you pray?'

"'No.'

"'What have you memorized from the Quran?'

"'*Say: He is God, the One.*'

"'Haven't you memorized the Fatiha?'

"'No.'

"'Why did you start with "*Say: He is God, the One*"?'

"'Because of its power to control the jinn,' I said.

"'Do you deal with the jinn?'

"'Yes. Many of them live in our storeroom and they fill Margush by night.'

"'Have you seen them with your own eyes?' he asked.

"'Often,' I said.

"'You are lying to your grandfather.'

"'I saw them and dealt with them,' I insisted.

"He gently passed his finger over the contour of my face. I felt close to him and got over my nervousness.

"'Do not lie, Jaafar. I do not like lies.'

"'I am telling the truth.'

18

"'Look with your eyes and do not imagine what does not exist.'

"'Grandfather,' I said.

"He looked at me inquisitively.

"'Why haven't you ever visited us?'

"He turned his gaze in direction of the garden. 'Your grandfather is old, as you can see.'

"'Why haven't you invited us to your house?'

"He was silent for a long time, then said, "Your father refused!'

"'Will I be living here for good?'

"'It is your house, Jaafar.'

"'Will I be able to play in the garden?'

"'You will, but your life will not be all play. You are six years old and you must begin to live.' And my new life began."

※

Jaafar stopped and said angrily to me, "That was my grandfather, al-Rawi, the owner of the waqf. What law deprives me of my legitimate right?"

"Let's return to your new life," I suggested.

"I am not an insignificant being, as you seem to think," he declared. "I have rights and I am educated. I can talk to you about the drawbacks of democracy and those of communism."

"You can talk to me about all this throughout your story, but do return now to your new life."

He shrugged and said, "What a shame—my eyesight is failing and I will lose it totally one day. There are not many years left for me to live. Human beings still endure pain and anxiety. We die, leaving behind a fulfilled but forgotten hope, and seven disappointments preoccupy us to the time of our death. And here you are, asking me to relate my life story according to the way you like it, rather than the way it suits me."

"We need to be organized so I can learn your life story in the few remaining days of your life."

He gave in to my pleadings and resumed his tale.

19

"My new life was a fascinating dream. I forgot the past. My ungrateful heart forgot my dead mother whose tomb I never visited. One night I dreamed of her, and when I woke up my heart was heavy and I cried. But young hearts find consolation very quickly. I was entranced by the stream and the henna trees, the palm and lemon trees, the vineyard, the frogs, the birds, the nightingales, the pigeons, and the doves. Even the furniture fired my imagination. I was fascinated by the copper utensils decorated with gold, the Persian rugs, the luxurious cupboard, the huge carved mirror, the colorful curtains, and the comfortable couches. There was also the balcony covered by English ivy and the large bathroom with its tiled floor and unusual water tank. I continually discovered new objects that were valuable and historical, and had new names and a gorgeous appearance. I was awed by this display of wealth, but never fell in love with it. It did not truly touch my heart.

"The needs of children were not taken into consideration when the palace was designed, which explains why I was most impressed by the gardener's donkey. I found a friend and a playmate in him, and spent long hours riding him back and forth in the alley, carefully avoiding the low-lying branches. I admired greatly the water pump, the well, the water fountain, and the peacock that stood on a marble pole in its center.

"A kind old copper-skinned woman called Bahga took care of me. It did not take long for us to bond. On various occasions, and over a rather long period of time, Bahga told me a great deal about the tragedy surrounding my birth. I discovered that my grandfather lived alone, surrounded by a retinue of servants. My grandmother had died a short time ago and my father had passed away far from the house. My father was the only son out of eight children who reached manhood. The other seven died, some in their childhood and others in their youth. He was the hope, after so much pain and the dream of the future; but that future, in my grandfather's opinion, resulted in a disappointment worse than death. Otherwise, he would not have had the courage to punish my father to such a degree, completely severing ties with him, exiling him like an enemy and excluding him from the house, the family, and the inheritance.

"All this contributed to making my grandfather a puzzle to me. His personality conveyed compassion, magnanimity, and sweetness, but anger transformed him into a devil or a hard stone. When I met him he was semi-retired in his house, but originally he was a graduate of al-Azhar, and inherited from his father and forefathers a huge fortune and a connection to that great university. Despite all that, he never worked in public office, either in a religious or a teaching position. His only activity was looking after the properties he owned. In his free time he read and studied religious and philosophical books, and works dealing with economics, politics, and literature. His reception hall was the meeting place of men of religion and Sufis, and those who were concerned with politics and literature."

✺

I asked him if his grandfather did writing of any sort.

"No," he said. "But he used to write down his daily activities in a journal. I know nothing about it, however."

"Was this the case with his father and grandfather?"

"They were counted among the reputable scholars of their time. He is the only one who chose to invest his wealth and run his business, and live without any constraint."

"Do you know who was the self-made man in the lineage of your ancestors? I mean, the poor man who was the source of this accumulated wealth?"

"It is an old family well-known for its wealth and piety," he said, then added, "I must be its first vagabond."

We both laughed, and he went on. "My father had a religious upbringing. He followed in the footsteps of previous family members and received his Alamiya degree from al-Azhar. He wanted to travel to Europe to visit and study. My grandfather hesitated a very long time before letting him go. In France, he studied French and attended lectures on philosophy and theology, though only to educate himself. He returned to Egypt without a degree and expressed his wish to help run the family business. My grandfather agreed.

"My father occasionally published articles in various newspapers. He fell in love with my mother as my grandfather was preparing to marry him to the daughter of the dean of al-Azhar. Unconcerned, my father married my mother. I do not know what problem my grandfather had with her. Perhaps it was her poverty. I must say that I never met any of her family members, an uncle or an aunt, close or distant relatives. In any case, old al-Rawi was extremely angry with his son. He repudiated him and broke all ties with him. It appeared to everyone that al-Rawi's lineage had ended, with all its historical significance. I have no doubt that my father could not care less about the al-Rawi lineage. He wanted to fulfill himself in a different way. I admired him for doing so and I felt sorry for his death, though I did not mourn him, since I was so young."

※

"Do you have an idea about the articles your father published in the press?" I asked.

"I looked them up in the archives of some newspapers. They call for the reconciliation between religion and science and philosophy. In all objectivity, I consider them timely and progressive, and I can generally classify my father as a liberal. I also learned that my father had been working as a translator for *al-Fagr* newspaper when he broke with his father. When I reached an age that permitted me to engage in discussions, I asked my grandfather, during an informal gathering, 'Grandfather, how did you find it in your heart to reject my father for marrying a woman who was a commoner? You are a religious man, of a pure soul and a noble nature. How could you do that?'

"Obviously, he was not thrilled by my question, but he answered me in these words: 'You are wrong in your interpretation. I put people in two categories: godly and worldly. The godly person lives in God's presence all the time, even if he is a highway robber; and the worldly person leads a worldly life, even if he is a man of religion.'

"'Was my father a bad man, then?' I asked.

"'He was only worldly.'

"'But my mother was good-hearted and noble.'

"'May her soul rest in peace,' he mumbled.

"He said, after a moment of silence, "I was not wrong and I never regretted my decision, but I was very sad for a long time.'

"Of this I was sure, and were it not for his deep sorrow, he would not have been compassionate with me. He went on, saying, 'I opened my heart and my home to you. Everything will be yours, but you must be a godly person. I am not asking you to become an ascetic. Here I am actively involved in running my business, looking after my real estate.'

"He immediately made arrangements for a tutor to teach me the principles of religion, mathematics, and Arabic. I was taught the notions of a religion, different from the one I learned from my mother. Hers was a religion of adventure, legends, miracles, dreams, and ghosts. But this was a religion that began with serious learning, the memorization of suras and their explanations, prayers and fasting and familiarity with rules. It was both a theoretical and an applied religion. The teacher was strict and gave my grandfather weekly reports. He was happy with my performance and told me so: 'You are a blessed boy. May you continue to be the subject of God's grace.'

"I had a powerful memory, quick understanding, and I loved to work. I was happy to pray and fast, confident in my grandfather. I did not forget my first religion, however, and the new teachings piled on top of the old notions. My mother's voice continued to echo deep inside me. In a discussion about a saint's tomb, my teacher said, 'It is only a building, and the saint is simply a corpse.'

"But I said, 'Everything has a life that never ends.'

"He said, smiling, 'Let's leave our misunderstandings to time and greater knowledge.'

"I must have achieved noticeable progress, because my grandfather began inviting me to attend his gatherings, which were frequented by some of the most prominent religious scholars and men of society. He would let me stay for a limited time in accordance with my education, but I often heard his guests praise my ancestors and their legendary positions, filling me with pride for those outstanding men who were known for their knowledge, their generosity, and their virtuous natures. I was saddened, however, by the absence of any mention of my father and the mystery that surrounded my mother's origin. The older I grew, the more painful her memory became. I was convinced that my parents' tragedy was contrary to the religious education I was receiving and practicing, and my grandfather acted sometimes like an unbeliever! My mother was gone, but I had inherited her religion and her tragedy, which would remain part of my inner self for a long time, longer than I ever imagined.

"My grandfather overwhelmed me with his love and tenderness, all the while keeping an eye on my progress and success. He said to me one day, 'Jaafar, I find you worthy of reviving the youth of our blessed family tree!' On another occasion, he told me, 'Walk hand in hand with wisdom and do whatever you want.' He also said, 'Blessed is he who surrounds himself with God's inspiration. The diligent person has the possibility to ascend the throne.' In a moment of optimistic elation, he declared, 'Your continued success is blessed, and you will be soon admitted to al-Azhar. Does this please you?'

"I replied, with all sincerity, 'It would please me greatly, Grandfather, and I would like to go to Europe later.'

"I could read a deep interest in his eyes as he wondered about the motivation behind my proposed European trip. 'I want to follow in my father's footsteps,' I said.

"Smoothing his long white beard, he muttered, 'You must first adorn yourself with God's inspiration; then you can do whatever you want.'

"'Was my father's marriage to my mother his only sin?' I asked, after a moment of hesitation.

"Looking gloomy, he said angrily, 'What is past is past.' Then he closed his eyes as if to release some of his resentment. He added, 'I have explained the situation to you, but you do not want to understand.'

"He looked sullen, but I saw something much worse than that, and it lasted more than a mere moment. It was a transformation of his appearance into a frightening person. His look was flinty, his facial muscles hardened, his color changed, and I had the impression I was looking at someone I had never seen before. He was like a foe launching out of a volcano's mouth and bearing the anger of the world, akin to a hurricane, or even to death itself. But after a short while, my grandfather returned to his usual self.

"Apart from that moment, he wasn't cruel, frightening, or unbearable. He exuded humanity and acted so lovingly that it was hard for me to believe he had treated my father the way he had. I often thought that he might have entertained forgiveness, waiting for the right time to pardon his son, had it not been for my father's early death. Even after I observed his frightening expression, I felt in his words, 'What is past is past,' the pain that the memory revived, and a remorse that haunted him. His suffering might have been the result of his exaggerated idealism, as he expected others to be noble, pure, and perfect, conforming to his vision of life. He despised weakness and what he considered to be the dissolution and degradation of human nature. I was thus convinced that the way to his affection was clear and straightforward, but required effort, patience, and sweat, in addition to strength, progress, and loftiness. This was what he meant when he referred to the 'godly human being.'

"During the religious festival seasons, his guests gathered to listen to the songs that filled the garden with Sufi chanting performed by the most famous singers. My grandfather was enamored of music and singing. His taste reflected his appreciation for the wordly and the sacred in equal measure. I waited for those soirées with the longing of a lover and stayed up till dawn to listen to the chants. My grandfather once caught me singing 'Bring Back the Memory of the One I Love.'

"I was sitting on a mat under a lemon tree, imitating the sheikh, when I noticed his shadow covering me. I stopped singing, extremely embarrassed and bashful. I stood before him politely, but he smiled and whispered, 'What is that? Your voice is not bad at all, Jaafar.'

"I lowered my head, contented and grateful. He asked, 'What do you sing when you are alone?'

"'Songs from the past,' I said.

"'Which ones?' he asked.

"I hesitated a little, then said, 'My Bird, Mother, My Bird.'

"He continued to smile and said, 'See, you are learning sacred songs here.' He then went on his way, checking the garden, looking august and dignified.

"During my free time I would sit with Bahga and listen to her stories. Sometimes I sang or rode the donkey in the garden, or played with the children of the gardener, the cook, and the carriage driver, but I longed to go out to play in the alley. How could I forget my trips in the narrow streets of Cairo, holding my mother's hand? When I shared with my grandfather my wish to go out, he invited me to join him in his carriage in the evening.

"I said, 'I want to play in the alley.'

"'Isn't the garden more beautiful than the alley?'

"'I want to play with the children, in the alley,' I explained.

"He shook his head and gave up. His acceptance was conditional, however. 'You must remain under Bahga's supervision all the time and not miss any of the prayer times.'

"So I went out to the street from where I came. Bahga sat on a chair in front of the door to watch me from a distance. I quickly became acquainted with the neighbors' children, and especially Muhammad Shakroun, the son of a cart driver. He was handsome, despite his big nose and his limp. He challenged me to a race on the first day we met. He looked funny when he ran, but he was stubborn and every now and then he took a devilish jump that propelled him over an unbelievably long distance, thus overcoming his natural weakness. He was kind and honest, and when he was declared the winner he said to me, 'You are the grandson of the venerable sheikh, and a wealthy boy like you must buy us red chewing gum and subiya.'

"After he ate and drank he was happy and began singing:

From the top of the mountain I hear a melody at night.
The love of virgin girls has exhausted me
From the top of the mountain.

"He had a beautiful, pure voice that moved the soul. I knew immediately I could not compete with him. Nevertheless, I sang whatever I could remember from his song. He repeated what my grandfather had already said, that my voice was not bad at all.

"'It is you, Shakroun, who has a truly beautiful voice,' I said.

"He replied proudly, 'One day I will become a famous singer.'

"We quickly became good friends, a true friendship among many superficial ones. Our friendship was deep and strong, and we shared a love for singing, especially during Ramadan nights. I invited him to attend the religious chanting soirées at my grandfather's house; it made him very happy. He was delighted to hear the famous singers and follow closely their prowess in chanting, the differences in their voices, and their ability to entertain and impress. I could see his strong emotional reaction, his passion and entrancement, and dared him to brave the dignity of the council. One day, no sooner had one singer ended his verse than Muhammad Shakroun left his place near me and began chanting, 'Welcome to a full moon, filled with the essence of beauty.'

"He captivated the chanters and the guests with his beautiful voice and his youth. My grandfather could not hide his admiration for him. There was among the guests a sheikh called Taher al-Bunduqi, a Sufi composer and a close friend of my grandfather. Shakroun impressed him greatly, and he talked with Shakroun at length. He learned everything about him, his origins and his dreams. This is the magic of singing. The jinn enjoy our songs and we do theirs. Some of Margush's inhabitants claimed that they heard a jinn sing before dawn and—"

I interrupted Jaafar, begging, "Let's forget about the jinn. We are now in al-Rawi's house and I am strongly convinced that you do not believe any of those stories."

27

"Memories pour heavily like rain," he said.

"They always do," I said, "but it is up to you to channel them into a clear stream."

He went on relating Shakroun's story.

"Sheikh Taher al-Bunduqi visited my grandfather a week after Shakroun's adventure and told him he wished to teach Shakroun oriental music and train him as a singer. My grandfather agreed immediately, and offered to pay for the lessons and the training. This convinced me of my grandfather's deep love for music and singing. It was a separate emotion, totally independent of his religious feelings. When he informed me of his decision to support my friend, I said to him, 'You do like singing, Grandfather.'

"He smiled and said, 'Why not? It is the soul's intimate friend.'

"'Have you heard the famous singers, Grandfather?'

"'Yes,' he said. 'In my friends' homes, during the celebration of happy occasions.'

"His financial support for Shakroun's music lessons was one example of how he took care of the needy in our district."

❋

I said impulsively, "Your grandfather topped all that by willing his real estate to charity."

"No," Jaafar said loudly, "that is not charity. Nothing good comes out of a charitable act based on evil."

"I apologize for the interruption," I said.

"It is more important to apologize for your opinion."

I did. He got over his ire, then continued.

"Muhammad Shakroun became Sheikh Taher al-Bunduqi's student. Our friendship brought him luck and I was the gate to his success. I was very happy for him, and I exaggerated my feeling of happiness when talking with my grandfather. He was suspicious of me, which made him ask, 'Is your happiness mixed with jealousy?'

"I denied any such feeling strongly.

"Dissatisfied, he said, 'Jealousy is a vice, and at your age you can be excused for your feelings, but there is no excuse for lying. Don't ever lie, Jaafar, always be truthful. Do not upset your grandfather, he likes purity. God gave you a bright mind the way He gave your friend a beautiful voice, so enjoy the gift you have been given and do not ruffle your serenity with what you lack. Had you been gifted at singing, I would not have minded you becoming a singer. A singer can be a godly human being. God's mercy makes it possible for anyone to be godly, even the garbage collector. As for you, Jaafar, you must get ready to enter al-Azhar.'

"I said, with all sincerity, 'My dearest wish, Grandfather, is to be successful in my religious life.'

"I can't deny that I felt slightly jealous of Shakroun, and it bothered me that my grandfather was able to penetrate my inner self with his great ability to read what was in my heart. In any case, I was jealous. Here was Shakroun excelling with a gift that did not require special diligence, while I was enduring conflicting feelings in my tortured heart. My dreams, however, revolved around religion and religious life, and I had a vague feeling that a certain mission was waiting for me in this sacred domain. I was eagerly looking forward to it, without losing sight of the huge inheritance that awaited me, the Marg farm, numerous buildings, and huge amounts of money. I was not concerned about work, but I dreamed of the mission, of sitting on my grandfather's bench and welcoming the men of the world and the men of religion, to discuss important topics with them, and relish the company of singers."

※

I interrupted him again. "I remember," I said, "the limping singer, as I remember you wearing the gibba and the quftan."

He said, boasting, "Then you saw how handsome God created me!"

"You were truly handsome."

"I was handsome," he said, "with a good reputation, and I had noble hopes. I enrolled in al-Azhar during my adolescence, filled with an enlightening power. I felt like a celestial prince and I found myself in an authentic environment, enduring poverty and sorrow, and deprived of true humanity, except through strict effort, sustained diligence, and the relentless acquisition of knowledge. I met a large number of peers and befriended many of them. Their folksy ways and their superstitions reminded me of Margush, of my mother's hand and my true tragic origin. I loved them despite everything, and invited them to my house for dinner every Friday evening. A select group among them used to eat iftar and suhur with me during the month of Ramadan. We spent the time between iftar and suhur studying and engaging in discussions. All that placed me in a unique position rarely experienced by a student. My grandfather noticed how I relished this role, and he was quick to warn me, 'Beware of conceit! Fill your heart with the love of those noble poor and always remember the blessings that God bestowed on you.'

"My excellent performance in my studies won me my grandfather's favor. The sheikh teaching theology praised me to my grandfather, and so did the professors of jurisprudence, syntax, and logic. All this delighted my grandfather, who told me that I would make an excellent sheikh, but added this recommendation to his compliment: 'What is more important than all this is for you to proceed firmly on the path of purity.'

"I told my grandfather about my future plans. 'I want to dedicate my life to religion, but I do not know exactly how yet. I have no inclination toward preaching or teaching.'

"'It does not matter at all,' he said. 'What counts for me are your pure will, your faith, and your love of religion. You will find out that every book is a book about religion and every location is a place of worship, whether in Egypt or in Europe. God will help you in your search for wisdom, to make you a provider of wisdom in words or in action. This is the godly life.'

"I was greatly motivated by his words and was pushing ahead with a heart filled with faith and piety, guided by my grandfather's example, his rich, beautiful life that I shared with him in his palace, meeting his friends and listening to his discussions and his songs and music. But I also experienced dark hours that sneaked up on me and changed the quality of my life. Clouds of black memories swept over me, reminding me of the rejection my father had endured and my mother's tragedy, my mother whose life remained mysterious and unknown to me. Whenever this happened, my anger against my grandfather would boil up and I would subject him to a severe judgment in my imagination. He would then appear like a devil disguised as an angel, a mere bourgeois enjoying the beautiful things in life, pretending to be a saint.

"The only person with whom I could share my feelings was Muhammad Shakroun. He was beginning to make a name for himself in a field crowded with established singers. He loved my grandfather and was grateful for his help, referring to him as 'a noble man, descendant of a noble family, unmatched among God's creatures.' Upon hearing those words I would ask him, 'What do you think of his attitude toward my parents?' His response came always in the form of a long tirade: 'The relationship of a father with his son is mysterious despite its superficial clarity. Sometimes it overflows with affection and sometimes it hardens as a result of cruelty. My limp was caused by my father in a moment of anger. The true conduct of a man can only be assessed in light of his relationship with others.'

"I was not convinced by his theory, and told him, 'The character of a man, any man, is whole and cannot be divided.'

"Though I was assailed by those dark moments, they were passing moments and not fixed opinions. I would return quickly to the serenity of my soul and the clarity of my vision. The true crisis I endured at this time was a sexual one, that of an adolescent longing for holiness but enduring a continual struggle with his strong natural instincts. I often remembered the wooden box and the girl, now totally unknown to me. I was extremely surprised by my grandfather, who discussed all kinds of ideas I had but was totally oblivious to the true battle raging inside me.

"There were three women in the house, in addition to old Bahga. They were in their fifties, and plain, but they possessed a remnant of charm that could attract a repressed adolescent. I even found the decently dressed women I saw on the street very provocative. I experienced continuous conflict between my conscience and my instincts, but was finally able to overcome temptation with a strong will worthy of admiration. It was as if my longing for God had over-taken everything else and defeated Satan in all his dwellings.

"Bahga was in fact concerned by my glances at her companions. From her position as my surrogate mother, she shared her concern with me, imploring, 'Do not disgrace yourself. Your grandfather considers every person in this house an extension of himself and views an infringement on their honors an infringement on his. You have so far enjoyed his approval, and you have certainly found that to be a true blessing, for which you should be grateful. There is another side to your grandfather, however, which you are well positioned to know.'

"Alarmed, I said, 'My father!'

"'Yes,' she replied. 'You are a true believer and your prayers are sincere. Why don't you think seriously about getting married? Your grandfather is capable of marrying you to a girl who would fulfill all your dreams and then some.'

"Her words came as a total surprise. 'I had not thought about that and I don't think this is the right time for it,' I said. 'I also reject the idea of marriage as a substitute for the fear of sin.'

"'I do not understand your thinking,' she said, 'but if you need help, I am ready to lend a hand.'

"I told Muhammad Shakroun, who was aware of my struggle and my dilemma, about that conversation. He had often wondered about my attitude, and had told me time and again, 'Come with me to the houses of the awalim. The gatherings in their homes provide wonderful opportunities for interaction. All you have to do is change your religious clothes in my house before you go there.'

"I laughed and refused all solutions with pride and dignity. I was happy to endure my pain and overcome it, saying to myself, 'Blessings be upon me. I defeat Satan at least once a day. I am truly worthy of my chaste future.'

"I turned my attention to other matters, and asked Bahga for the first time about my grandmother: 'When did she die?'

"'May her soul rest in peace,' she said, 'she died almost twenty years ago.'

"'Did my father's tragedy have anything to do with her death?'

"'Only God decides a person's death.'

"'Why didn't my grandfather remarry after her death?' I asked.

"'That's his business.'

"I wondered about my grandfather's sexual life, but shivered at the strangeness of the idea. I said to myself that, as usual, he would read my thoughts in my eyes and a new tragedy would occur. I thought that part of me was pursuing my grandfather with an inclination for revenge. This meant that my love for him was not whole, but was tainted by my inability to completely forget my father's tragedy. I persisted with my questions to Bahga, until she admitted that my mother had been the daughter of a peddler who frequently visited the house. I asked if she was a woman of ill repute, which she denied, saying, 'Your grandfather does not acknowledge anonymous people!'

"I was resentful, and objected: 'But all people, with very few exceptions, are anonymous. He dreams of a world filled with "divine beings," as he says, but isn't he aware of the cruelty of his dream?'

"I decided to fast during the three months of Rajab, Shaaban, and Ramadan every year. My life was one of endeavor, diligence, and purity, followed closely and attentively by my grandfather. He would often say to me, 'God's will is great.'"

5

I was walking with Muhammad Shakroun at the edge of al-Darrasa when we encountered a herd of sheep led by two women. When we stepped aside to let them pass, I was able to see the women up close, most probably a mother and a daughter, very much alike. The daughter wore a long belted black dress, was draped in a black shawl, and had on a loose burqa that revealed her eyes. She was barefoot and held a spindle."

Jaafar fell silent for a long time.

"What happened?" I asked.

He turned toward me and said, "I, too, wonder what happened."

"What do you mean?"

He went on: "To sum it up, I looked at the girl's eyes and was struck by a state of total madness. But let's leave this for the time being and discuss it later. I will tell you now what happened. I felt I had died and that a new person was born through me. You will even agree with me that it was a new person in the full meaning of the word, a person with no connection to the one who had just died, a drunkard whose heart overflowed with passion and who had an extraordinary capacity for defiance and struggle. I heard Muhammad Shakroun say, 'When will you resume walking?' He then examined me closely and smiling, said, 'It must be the shepherdess!'

"'It's fate,' I replied.

"'What are you thinking?' he asked.

"'We must find out where she lives.'

"'Fine,' said Shakroun, 'but remember that you are wearing a turban.'

"A force of another kind guided me. We walked behind the herd, crossing al-Nahhasin district, then al-Husseiniya, and then I saw al-Abbasiya and al-Wayliya. I did not feel any fatigue and I had no pity for my friend's limp, but walked extremely fast, like a crazy, intoxicated man. The springs of adventure overwhelmed my heart, though Muhammad Shakroun uttered a litany of complaints.

"'May God forgive you,' he said.

"'What's wrong with you?' I asked.

"'The girl is aware that you are following her.'

"'These are gypsies; they're worse than devils,' I said.

"'Tell me, I beg you, what exactly do you want?' asked Shakroun.

"We finally saw the herd enter the campground of Eshash al-Turguman, as the sun's rays were withdrawing from that eerie open space and disappearing at the horizon. The rays were bidding good-bye to the metal-roofed huts and their wild inhabitants, with their nomadic life so different from that of city dwellers. Muhammad Shakroun stopped and grabbed my arm.

"'Not a single step farther,' he said. 'There is no place for a stranger here.' He added, 'You have bloodied our feet.'

"I was floating in a distant sphere, the world of emotions, as I said to Shakroun, 'She bid me good-bye with a fiery look before disappearing.'

"'Congratulations!'

"He begged me to hire a carriage for the return trip.

"Shakroun did not leave me that evening, staying till midnight and watching me in disbelief. 'What happened to you?'

"I said in distress, 'You see with your own eyes.'

"'I don't understand.'

"'I am crazy about the girl,' I said.

"'So fast?'

"'It happened.'

"'But she is a shepherdess and belongs to an evil group of people!' he exclaimed.

"'It is destiny and there is no escaping it,' I replied.

"He went on, wondering, 'How can she be seduced? Would she be inclined to that? How can we arrange matters without causing a scandal? What can you do if none of that is possible?'

"I insisted, saying, 'No matter what, I must have her.'

"From that day on I spent sunsets at the edge of al-Darrasa, with my friend or alone, sitting on a rock and surrounded by grazing sheep and goats, with the book of logic open on my lap. I caught glimpses of her as she sat close to her mother, weaving. The place was practically empty, frequented only by vagrants returning to the Muqattam neighborhood. When the sun set, the herd and its herders went on their daily return journey, leaving me with a gloomy and empty heart. I would leave and go to the mosque for the evening prayer, and then attend my lesson on the subject of logic.

"One day I hid a glass in my caftan pocket, and as they reached the place where I sat, I walked to the mother and gave her the glass, asking for some milk. Marwana, as I heard her mother call her, jumped immediately to her feet, went to a goat, and milked it. She handed me the glass full of foaming milk. I took it and thanked her, saying, 'May your hands be safe, Marwana.' She smiled with her eyes. Her mother looked at me suspiciously as I drank the milk and said, 'To your health.' When I thanked her, she replied in a tone that carried a specific message, 'You sheikhs are God's people.' I said, grateful, 'Thanks be to God.'

"I was delighted to have established this contact and struck up a conversation with them. I was overcome with a tremendous feeling of happiness that lasted until the moment of separation.

"Shakroun, who was investigating possible solutions, reached the following conclusion: 'I inquired enough to know that this group commits every kind of evil except the one that you are drooling about.'

"I said scornfully, 'A giant will come out of the lamp one day and you will not recognize him no matter how strongly you claim to have been his friend.'

"Shakroun was not aware of the revolutionary nature of my words. He didn't know that I had become the king of kings and could do whatever I wanted. I was intoxicated with an outpouring of red madness.

"The glass of milk established a silken but fatal link between Marwana and me. When I again asked for milk, I accidentally touched her fingertips as I took the glass from her and said, 'You are generous, Marwana!'

"She gathered her veil around her head and glanced at me mischievously. I said to her very softly, 'Your eyes are so beautiful!' As she was turning away, I added, 'I come here for you only.'

"The mother stopped weaving and stood up. Taking a pebble from the ground, she threw it far away, in the direction of the mountain. As I watched her, surprised, she explained, 'It is a good way to scare away reptiles and insects.'

"I said, distrustfully, 'God is the best protector.' She replied forcefully, 'It is incumbent upon us to fight evil with the language it understands.'"

Jaafar laughed and said to me, "Believe everything I am telling you without hesitation. Do not be fooled by my present appearance. Whoever sees me now thinks that I was born in a dumpster and my only actions have been those connected to vomiting. Tell me, what do you think of love?"

I was taken aback by the difficult nature of the question and said, "Love is what it is. I believe everything people say about it."

"Do you also believe that it is a miracle maker and produces wonders?" he asked.

"I do. I am not a greenhorn, but tell me about your love, Jaafar. How was it? A barefoot shepherdess is bound to make one's blood boil!"

Jaafar confirmed my words. "That is how it was: a call for blood, a loud call that led to action, to madness and destruction. It invaded one's life through doors and windows and led to crimes and suicide."

Surprised, I said, "But you were one of God's holy men."

"In order to understand my experience, imagine that you suddenly lost your memory and became a new person."

"I thought that a person changes gradually."

"Not me. I change from one extreme to another, suddenly!"

I offered an explanation. "Many things can, undoubtedly, happen in the obscure regions of your subconscious."

He had his own explanation. "Man invents logic, but surpasses it in his life. Nature, my dear man, makes use of impetuosity as well as evolution!"

"Go on. Let me hear what you have to say, Jaafar."

He continued: "One day, my grandfather invited me to sit with him, then inquired about my studies. I understood immediately that he had asked me to join him for another reason, since my teachers were informing him about my exceptional progress. I reassured him about my earnestness and my aim to always please him. 'But the road is long and full of hardships,' he said. I replied with affected enthusiasm, 'A believer is not deterred by the road ahead.'

"'Fine words, but good deeds are more important than fine words.'

"'This is true.'

"He hesitated for a few seconds then said, 'There are things that call for some consideration. I had a dream, and when I woke I made up my mind to do something about it.'

"'What is that dream, Grandfather?' I asked.

"'It is of no importance, and dreams are easily forgotten, but what counts is the decision I made.'

"I asked if it concerned me. 'Of course,' he said, 'and you will be happy with it. I decided to marry you to an honorable girl.'

"I was shocked and dumbfounded. I told myself that the man knew everything. How had I ever thought that an unusual evening stroll by al-Rawi's grandson wouldn't attract attention and provoke comments? Many would volunteer to inform my grandfather. He definitely knew everything and was trying to salvage what he could.

"'Anything wrong, my son?' he asked.

"'The idea had not crossed my mind,' I replied.

"'Think about it then.' And he added, 'A number of young men do not marry, for reasons beyond their control, but God has given you the means to marry. So what is the point of delaying what is considered half your religious duty?'

"'Give me time to think about the matter.'

"'I will choose an exceptional bride and will let you decide.'

"I went back to my room in a state of extreme anger, unable to sleep. I heard the dawn call to prayer and felt a surge of enormous energy, with a strong desire to attack the walls and destroy them. The giant inside me was released and eager for confrontation, determined to get his girl at the expense of the whole neighborhood, not just the palace. I invoked my mother and my father, and my anger against my grandfather was limitless as I considered his continual tendency to control and repress others. In my state of perplexity, as conflicting thoughts fought for control, a dialogue began between me and my grandfather. I can't be sure whether it was in a dream, a delusional condition of the night, or a state between sleep and awakening. I said to him, 'Grandfather, I refuse.'

"'You turn down my generosity?'

"'I am against repression.'

"'Even coming from me?'

"'Even from you.'

"'You are ungrateful. You turn down beauty and purity in exchange for what?'

"'Freedom!'

"'The shepherdess,' he said.

"'I follow the call of blood, the life of a vagabond, and fresh air.'

"'It is rather the madness that leads the crazy individuals out of my old house.'

"'True felicity is in a state of madness,' I told him.

"'You are your parents' child.'

"'I will take pride in that forever.'

"'Part of you wants to take revenge on me.'

"'I do not want to think, so let me act.'

"'What about your clothing, the gibba and the quftan?'

"'I will get rid of them immediately.'

"'You are reneging, then!'

"'I do not want religion to be a profession.'

"'What do you want to do then?'

"'I want to practice love, madness, and murder!'

"I believe that through this dialogue I clearly expressed my feelings. When I shared my secrets with Muhammad Shakroun, he was shocked, and could not believe his ears. When he understood that I was serious, he asked me, 'Do you truly turn down your grandfather's offer for Marwana's sake?'

"I replied affirmatively. But he went on, 'Would you leave the house for the sake of a shepherdess?'

"'I would.'

"He asked again, 'What does this all mean?'

"I told him, 'Consider me crazy if you want.'

"He was concerned: 'Don't you fear that he'll deprive you of your inheritance and you'll end up a pauper?'

"'It's possible,' I said.

"'No woman deserves such a huge sacrifice,' said Shakroun. I took his words lightly, making fun of them. 'I do not understand you,' he said.

"'There is nothing to understand,' I said. 'It is reality.'

"'How do you explain it? Is there a secret?'

"'It is a splendid madness, and I am mesmerized by it.'

"He advised me to be patient, in hopes of finding a compromise, but I objected, saying that I disliked compromise. He offered another solution: 'You can remain in your grandfather's care. Pursue your education and experience your mad love.'

"'No. No. These are very contradictory matters and I have made my choice.'

"'What have you chosen?'

"I informed him of my decision to leave my grandfather's house as well as al-Azhar. He said it was not necessary, so I explained my position. 'It is imperative. I will lead a new life. Otherwise, I will be expelled from both places.' Shakroun was convinced I had been hit by the evil eye, so I explained further: 'Only a divine person can live in my grandfather's house. As for al-Azhar, I never wanted to turn it into a profession. Faith does not require all these complications.'

"Saddened, Shakroun commented, 'I wish you were abandoning all that for something better.'

"I told him, 'Adventure is much better, and so is madness.' He said he would never understand me, and I said, sarcastically, 'Despite your follies, Shakroun, you have not known madness yet.'

"He asked, 'Does that mean that you are abandoning your past because of love?'

"'It is because of love that I have known madness in adventure!'

"Muhammad Shakroun finally gave in to reality. I sensed that he truly believed the tragedy did not lack real madness. He felt obligated to promise to help me determine Marwana's and her mother's inclination, saying that a lover needed support from a singer. His investigations confirmed for him that a person like Marwana would rather be killed than accept an illegitimate relationship. He asked me, annoyed, 'What about your future? Even free adventurers need to eat.'

"Strangely, I had not given the matter the attention it deserved. For a moment I considered teaching Arabic and religion in a public school, but soon abandoned the idea. It clashed with the magical nature of my adventure. I replaced it with another idea—forming a singing group to interpret tawashih praising the Prophet. Shakroun gave me an honest assessment of my chances in that field.

"'A long time would pass before you could hold such an evening, and your success is not guaranteed and requires hard work. The traditional way is to begin as a member in a group—something that does not suit you.'

"I thought about the matter and said, 'I prefer to work in your band.'

"'My band!' he said, surprised.

"'Why not? My voice is better than any of your support singers.'

"He said, 'I owe you a lot, but . . .'

"I did not give him a chance to finish his sentence. 'No buts, please. You entertain at parties at least one-third of the month, and are becoming better known every day.'

"Muhammad Shakroun fell silent, which encouraged me to tell him with great enthusiasm, 'My desire to form a religious band will not wane. I will do it at the same time.'

"'This is important,' said Shakroun. 'And you can count on my friendship with the agents of the religious ceremonies. I can't believe what we are planning; it is like living a dream. But I still say that it would be possible to deal with the matter in a different way.'

"'I will not go back even one step,' I insisted. 'I will have two outfits: a costume for your ceremonies and the gibba and the quftan for the religious band. Isn't this amazing!'"

Jaafar looked at me in the quiet of the night and asked, "How much do you believe me?"

"I am old enough to believe anything," I said.

"I want a stronger commitment," he said. "Many are those who did not believe me, which both hurt and gratified me. I was hurt

41

because innovative work requires witnesses, and I was happy to see my enterprising spirit acknowledged. I demand that people recognize me as an exceptional human being. It is my right to demand that. Few are capable of abandoning the lavish life I enjoyed, as swiftly as I did."

"Was all this for love alone?" I asked.

He replied, disapprovingly, "Isn't love sufficient? Love is creative madness!"

"Was Marwana so beautiful?"

"What is beauty?" he wondered. "The matter is a call that activates an electric key."

"Didn't you also want to deprive your grandfather of his only heir?"

"I never forgot my father's tragedy, but my decision was pure, free of any hidden or declared desire for revenge."

I ventured a second explanation: "Was it a reaction to the severe restrictions you imposed on yourself as a divine human being?"

He objected. "I refuse this explanation as well. I told you that it was an angelic move, like a song at dawn. Love ignited the spark, and its light revealed a dream that was taking shape, ready to raze the walls of the palace. It was getting ready to live, to confront wealth and restrictions and wallow in the dust of the eternal mother, like Buddha, who left his palace one day for a reason no one around him understood. These things happen suddenly and are not the result of a process of evolution, as you seem to think. It is a practical confirmation of a sudden creativity. I will give you a live example that took place at this exact instant: I have just decided against writing the petition."

"What do you mean?"

He explained that he was referring to the petition concerning the monthly financial support from his grandfather's waqf.

"Is this a return to a futile court case?" I asked.

"There will be neither a case nor a petition," he replied.

I objected, and asked him to postpone discussing this question and carry on with his story. He laughed loudly as usual, and continued to narrate his story.

"One evening Muhammad Shakroun, limping, and I behind him, approached the old Bedouin woman sitting in her tent. When she saw Shakroun, she put aside her weaving tool and stood up, fearful. He said to her, 'My friend would like to marry your daughter according to God's laws.'

"The woman was shocked. Marwana ran far from the tent while Muhammad Shakroun was saying, 'We are at your service.' When she regained control of herself, she told him, 'We have people we need to consult.'

"They had a distant relative we had to meet. It was a strange day. We were the first two strangers to enter Eshashal-Turguman in plain daylight without being killed. Some evil eyes stared at us, mockingly inquisitive and defiant. All activities stopped for a short while: the training of the monkeys, the herding of sheep, the weighing of drugs, the polishing of stolen goods, and the beating of drums. A group of children surrounded us and greeted us, chanting,

'Pull the turban, pull.
Under the turban is a monkey.'

"We proceeded to meet a man sitting in front of his hut, while Marwana's mother stood beside him. We greeted the very old man, who seemed on the verge of death, and Marwana's mother talked on his behalf. 'He welcomes you,' she said.

"The old man hit her on the back and said, 'You are damned because you consent to this.'

"Muhammad Shakroun said to him, 'My friend is from a respectable family.'

"'Tuzz,' said the old man after he spat.

"Embarrassed, Muhammad Shakroun added, 'He has also a job.'

"The old man interrupted him, saying, 'We do not care about a job either!'

"'His conduct—' began Shakroun, only to be interrupted again by the old man, saying, 'Neither do we care about conduct.'

"Showing a great deal of patience, Shakroun said, 'In a few words, we would like to ask for your girl's hand according to the laws of God and the Prophet.'

"The old man laughed, revealing a toothless mouth. 'Good riddance, but talk about her dowry.'

"Shakroun invited him to indicate the amount out of respect for his old age. Feeling important, the old man declared, 'I want ten pounds placed in my hand.' He stretched his hand out as he talked, provoking an angry reaction from Marwana's mother, but the old man frowned and said, 'Let's read the Fatiha.' Joyful ululations erupted everywhere around us.

"Sensitive to my feelings, Muhammad Shakroun did not make a single comment, and I decided to inform my grandfather of the truth, like any young man who has come of age and has completed an important part of his education. I sat close to his couch in the salamlik as he held a rosary in his hand, glorifying God, and his Siamese cat purring by his side. I felt an air of expectation and apprehension settle between us, provoked by my hidden intentions and his ability to discern people's thinking. He asked his usual question: 'How are you doing?'

"I replied absentmindedly, 'I am fine, thanks be to God.'

"He went on, 'The engagement will be made public in three months, after Ramadan.'

"I decided to try my newfound strength without delay, and said, 'Sorry, Grandfather, but I have chosen another wife.'

"'Really?' he said, without betraying any reaction.

"'It is God's will, anyhow,' I explained.

"'What I heard then is true?' he said.

"When I did not reply, he added, 'A shepherdess?'

"I said simply, 'Yes, Grandfather.'

"His only comment was: 'You have reached the age of reason and you know where your interest lies.'

"I asked if he would bless my choice, but he went on praising God on his rosary. I asked if this meant I had to leave the house. Without turning to me, he said, 'Forever.'

"I immediately kissed his hand and left.

"Saying good-bye to Bahga was tearful and painful. She suggested asking my grandfather for money, but I told her that I had saved more than a hundred pounds. She cried, saying, 'Sorrows in this house begin with marriage.' She then whispered in my ear, 'Believe me, your grandfather is a very unfortunate man. He rarely sleeps more than one hour at night.'

"I told her sincerely, 'I love him and I reject him.'

"I then left the house where I had lived for fourteen chaste years.

"I moved into a new two-bedroom apartment located in al-Khurunfish with my bride. Muhammad Shakroun helped me rent it and furnish it. Marwana was stunning in her wedding dress. I saw her true skin color for the first time, after the intensive cleaning she had undergone in the special bridal bath. I can't say that I was thrilled with the change, as I had gotten used to her metallic skin color, which was such an integral part of the image that had turned my life upside down. Nevertheless, I was strongly attracted to her, and totally enthralled by her. I felt I was a prisoner, at the mercy of a brutal power that knew no pity or clemency. She was instinctively seductive, like a tongue of fire. She was proud and she exalted her people, enrobing them with holiness, enriching the modest environment where she grew up like a wildflower. Even her feminine shyness was like a transparent veil, and not at all a sign of innate weakness or natural indolence. I immediately became aware that I was in the company of a strong, ageless woman, a source of fascination, charm, and defiance. I surrendered to her, clearly revealing my own weakness. I acted like a hunted man, or a crazy man who had thrown his senses and his caution to the wind. My new companions nicknamed me 'the happy man' and 'the weak happy man.' I was overwhelmed with warnings and advice.

"I did not forget my new work during my honeymoon, and I approached it with great energy and some apprehension. I was moving into new surroundings and mixing with people whose serious activities in life were fun and games. They would greet me, saying, 'Welcome to al-Rawi's grandson.'

"That greeting followed me like my shadow everywhere I went. I heard it in al-Khurunfish, in Muhammad Shakroun's band, and among the members of the choir that had agreed to work with me when needed. I applied myself to studying and training, quickly getting ready for the music band and the choir. Even during my honeymoon, I performed with the band to celebrate a wedding in al-Darb al-Ahmar, and I had to wear a suit and a fez for the first time in my life. When Muhammad Shakroun saw me, he said admiringly, 'May God be praised for his creation.'

"I was nervous as I walked into the midst of the guests and onlookers. I was one of only two members of the band who relied solely on his voice, without a musical instrument in my hand. Muhammad Shakroun offered me a glass of wine. 'A must,' he explained, 'if you do not want your voice to fail.'

"I became acquainted with wine and narcotics in the same week, and I sang forcefully and accurately, as I was the second-best voice in the choir. I infused new life into the band, and boosted its enthusiasm as I sang, 'I miss you so much, you're my life.'

"Our singing was well received. A drunk guest made an allusion to my condition and shouted, 'A scholar can produce a dissolute man,' provoking loud laughter among the guests. Muhammad Shakroun turned to me and whispered, 'Laugh with them.'

"Afterward, I thought about the man's words, and realized that people believed I was a good sheikh who'd gone astray, becoming a singer in a band, drinking wine and taking drugs. This was not the case. All I did was change my profession; instead of teaching and preaching, I sang. As for my soul, it rose a few degrees higher. My heart was not corrupt and my faith was not shaken. My grandfather himself had said that even a garbage collector could be a divine creature.

"I might have been transported at that time by the raging flood of my feelings, because I was not aware of the significance of my experience then as I was later, or as I am today. Despite that, I was upset by the drunk's comment, and saw in it an unfair and boisterous joke. In any case, I began my new work with confidence and success, but I waited a long time before I began chanting tawashih in praise of the Prophet at the head of a respectable group. My happiness in my marriage was the most important thing in my life, and had priority over success in my work. I was proud of my marriage, praised it, and shared the secrets of a happily married life and its benefits with others. I became an example to emulate.

"At the height of my happiness, I failed to look at my family critically, or even with a neutral probing eye. I welcomed the first signs of motherhood with a feeling close to religious ecstasy. There are, in all honesty, moments of betrayal even during a time of pure happiness; moments when you detach yourself from the flow of your life, when you stand on a hill overlooking a beach and observe it in total ecstasy. During those moments I felt as if someone had fooled me and I wondered what had happened. I would look at Marwana baffled, desiring strongly to take revenge on her. I couldn't explain that feeling. It was as if I hated her suddenly, for no reason. It generally lasted but a fleeting moment, like the sudden contraction of a muscle, after which life regained its happy course, surrounded by fiery passion.

"I was surprised by my ability to live in a messy house. I did not complain about Marwana's inability to cook or keep a tidy, clean house; how she went about the house half-naked and disheveled, defiant and ready to quarrel with the wind. She would frequently take my hand and drag me to visit her mother and her aging relative, living in the devils' camp.

"The senile old man would either laugh at me, saying, 'Wouldn't it have been better for you to be an imam in a mosque?' Or he would bless my wife's belly, telling the unborn child, 'Honor us by becoming a killer. We are fed up with thieves and smugglers.' He made fun of my noble origins on occasion, saying, 'Your grandfather is not al-Rawi. I am your true grandfather. I donated this beautiful woman to you, the woman who sucks up your devilish instincts.'

"'My grandfather is a man of God,' I would say in defense, but he would laugh at me, saying, 'We are the true men of God, the vengeful, powerful God, creator of hell and earthquakes. Look at these wastrels. They are the men of God, an image of God in His might and vengefulness.'

"One day I met my mother's neighbor in Bayn al-Surayn. She did not recognize me, but I introduced myself to her. She was surprised and wished me well. I remembered then that I did not know my mother's name, and neither did Bahga. I used to call my mother 'Amma,' and that was the name she answered to until the day she died. I asked the neighbor if she knew her name. 'May her soul rest in peace, she was called Sakina,' she said. I was tempted to ask more questions about my mother's origin and her life, but I repressed my desire, out of respect for her memory. I shook hands with the neighbor and went on my way. Thus I learned my mother's name by pure accident.

"Marwana and I had four sons, but the flame of passion faded away. I liked it when people said that I had abandoned a life of comfort for love and freedom. I appreciated Marwana's love for the short, lively songs Muhammad Shakroun's group sang and I forgave her dislike for the tawashih I prepared for my own group. I struggled against poverty with hard work, wine, and narcotics, a fight that kept me busy from dawn to dawn. It was a life of slavery!

"Then came the days of drought, aversion, and cruelty. Marwana became confrontational, verbally and physically abusive, as if she was born to fight. I told her once, 'A man has to be respected.'

"'And so does the woman!' She then added cruelly, 'There are no men outside Eshashal-Turguman.'

"Saddened, I asked, 'Is this how you reward the man who provided you with a beautifully furnished home?'

"'I hate the smell of houses!' she shouted.

"We dived deeper into the days of drought and cruelty. Muhammad Shakroun watched my condition with sorrow. He said to me, 'I dread mad love and prefer moderation.'

"I replied, feeling sadder than he could ever have guessed, 'I am the victim of blind desire.'

"'Married life necessarily goes through periods of trouble that require the wisdom of experts,' he said.

"'I have entered the zone of desperation!' I said, despondent.

"I realized that this partnership had turned into a battle that was fought covertly at times and overtly at other times. I became aware that once Marwana was stripped of her madly provocative inclinations, she was reduced to nothing, nothing at all. She became like a she-wolf. Whenever she was furious she destroyed everything she could reach, tore my clothes, threw my songbook out the window, and attacked me physically. During those moments I told her that I hated her more than I hated death, and she told me that she hated me more than an oozing sore.

"Those periods of deep hatred often lasted a long time, and peace was usually reestablished by the intervention of the children. Then desire would revive for brief moments, recalling the memory of our dreams, but only from a very distant past."

I asked him with great interest, "What really destroyed your marriage?"

"Haven't I made that clear?" he said.

"No, not as far as I'm concerned," I replied. "I still need specific reasons."

He said, "It was a state of madness that attached me to her. Once I passed this condition, I found myself with a woman I did not know and had no reason to be with. My general attitude must have betrayed my hidden feelings and upset her."

"The state of madness ends, but the children remain," I said.

"The children prolonged the life of my marriage but did not protect it from devastation. Marwana was only a sexual provocation; not a housewife, a mother, or a woman in the true sense of the word. Her genuine qualities would better suit a man and even a highway robber."

"What about her—didn't she love you?" I asked.

"I don't think so. It might have been a mad, passing emotion or a curious adventure to her. I did not represent the man she dreamed of. Our marriage brought together two adventurers, and it was doomed to fail the moment the adventure turned into a life of routine. I guess this is clear now."

I agreed with him, and he continued his narrative. "I, too, had my hidden dreams. I wished to escape from reality, from the house. I

49

wished to be alone, and even my children did not inhabit my dreams. But I did not know where to go. My work did not leave me time to look ahead, as tawashih chanters do not have a role model to emulate. Besides, God did not grant me the ability to be content and accept my fate. I was not the only one dreaming. Marwana was also dreaming. After one of our fights she remained angry and refused all attempts at reconciliation. She even confronted me, saying coldly, 'We must reconsider our life.'

"I heard in her tone a strong determination that depressed me. I mumbled, 'Our life?'

"'Frankly,' she said, 'it is unfair to remain together any longer.'

"I heard the voices of the children from a distance and listened sadly to them. Then I told her, 'All couples do that.'

"She replied, with frightening calm, 'But I want to leave.'

"'Where to?' I asked stupidly.

"'To be with my family.'

"I controlled myself and said, despite my anger, 'Don't you like living in this house?'

"'No, I do not,' she said. 'You think that we owe you—this is your problem.'

"'But I sacrificed a lot for you,' I said.

"'I am your first victim.'

"'Listen,' I said, then stopped to avoid fighting.

"She said loudly, 'I hate this life with all my heart!'

"I kept saying, 'What about the children, the children?'

"'I have the right to take them with me.'

"'Do you want them to grow up in Eshashal-Turguman?'

"'I want them to grow up to be men!'

"I told her that she was crazy, but she returned the insult, saying, 'You're the crazy one, and I can swear to that. No sane man lives from the use of his voice like a woman does.'

"There was no use arguing with her, but when she asked to go, I insisted on keeping the children.

"'What would you do with them?' she asked. 'You wake up in late afternoon and do not·return home till dawn or even later, and in a terrible state. How can they survive? Do you mean what you say?'

"Defeated, I said, 'That is why this house must remain open for their sake.'

"She objected, and the conversation did not lead to any solution.

"I thought of the children and realized that they couldn't live with me. I had to be patient for their sake, no matter how hard it was for me. But Marwana settled the matter in her own way: I returned home at dawn one day to find the house empty. Not a single soul was there. I went immediately to Eshashal-Turguman, reaching it early in the morning. Marwana's mother met me; she was in a sulky mood.

"'Go away peacefully,' she said, 'and do what men do for once!'

"'What about the children?' I said.

"'They are our children!' she replied disdainfully.

"Then the old man arrived, surrounded by a band of fierce-looking men. He addressed me, saying, 'You are a failure. Go back home.'

"The men muttered vague words, and I became aware of the danger I faced. The old man spoke again. 'Divorce her and give her all her rights, and if the sharia gives you rights now or later, I advise you to give them up if you want to save your skin. Leave before the sun shines on your face. I might commit a heinous crime if I see it in daylight.'

"I left immediately, and began the divorce process. I postponed thinking about the problem of my children, telling myself I would wait until my oldest reached the legal age when I could reclaim him. It was an escape. I knew very well that I wouldn't seriously try to claim my children since that would mean confronting a people who supplied Cairo with its violent criminals. It would also mean bringing them to a life where they could not possibly be cared for. Those children, descendants of al-Rawi, were destined to be lost wherever they went. Their only hope was in the radical salvation of the whole society.

"This is the way Marwana left me, taking with her a story of love, madness, and failure, a story of emotional drought and hatred. Nothing was left of it but the memory of an amazing desire, the power of confrontation, and obstinate arrogance. It was like a storm: frightening, destructive, and worthy of admiration. After the loss of the children, I was overcome with a sadness that wedged into the depths of my soul and settled in the room of sorrow, joining the memory of my mother and my father.

"I could not carry on living as if nothing had happened. Muhammad Shakroun felt sorry for me and watched over me carefully. One day, he asked me, 'How long will you go on singing, drinking wine, and taking drugs?'

"When Marwana and the children were living with me, my life had a semblance of normality, regardless of the quality of that life. Now, Shakroun's question was reasonable. I replied, without meaning what I said, 'Until death.'

"He said, very seriously, 'It is time for you to return to your grandfather.'

"'Sheikh Jaafar al-Rawi is finished.'

"'He can start all over again. We have to try,' said Shakroun.

"'I refuse to try.'

"'Is it pride?' asked Shakroun.

"'I am simply being realistic.'

"'What kind of reality is this?'

"'It is not my favorite choice, but I have categorically and definitively given up the religious life. The life that my grandfather planned for me is totally unacceptable, and he won't take me back unless I return to it.'

"'He might give you your personal freedom,' Shakroun said.

"'He won't. You do not know him like I do. I refuse to submit to a demeaning experience.'

"Shakroun said sincerely (and I never doubted his feelings), 'You are a dear friend, and it is my duty to tell you honestly that you are leading a life unworthy of you. You are neither a singer nor a composer, and you must consider your future more seriously.'

"'I can do that without living with my grandfather.'

"'You do not seem to be happy now.'

"'Maybe,' I said, 'but I embarked on a crazy adventure I will always be proud of. I am proud of the fact that I can adapt to any kind of life without complaint or weakness. You find me full of hope whether I live the life of a prince or a pauper. Here I am, holding on to the life of a pauper, and I refuse to go back to live in the palace. I refuse to be a respectable sheikh and a noble husband; to live by the fine traditions and norms not out of my own free will, but to fulfill my grandfather's vision and enticed by the inheritance.'

"'What about your future?' asked Shakroun.

"'I am thinking seriously about studying music and composition with Sheikh Taher al-Bunduqi. I can't go through my life without a goal.'

"Marwana was the symbol of a past life, and an excuse to live a normal life without a goal. When she left I found myself adrift; I had to rethink my life. It was at this critical time that I met Huda Sadeeq."

6

At a soirée in the Lipton Garden where Muhammad Shakroun was entertaining we were invited to meet Huda Sadeeq in her loge during the intermission. She received us with a smile that reflected her self-confidence. A very dark-complexioned woman sat beside her, and from her extreme politeness I guessed she was Huda Sadeeq's lady-in-waiting.

"I was struck by Huda's beauty, her conservative but elegant dress, and a certain pride that remained within the boundaries of politeness. She was enveloped in a halo of serious charm, but her feminine beauty was all in her eyes and her round face. I was certain that she was in her forties.

"She made a good impression on me, as I stood among the older members of the group, a healthy and tall young man, proud of my new suit. She invited us to sit down and ordered refreshments for us. She praised Muhammad Shakroun with these words,

"'Your voice is pure and your group is excellent. I belong to a family that adores beautiful voices.'

"Shakroun thanked her profusely and mentioned her late father, whom artists remembered very well, in flattering terms.

"'I have often heard my teacher, Sheikh Taher al-Bunduqi, say that your father's palace was the home of eastern music.'

"She smiled approvingly and our eyes met more than once. Shakroun introduced me proudly: 'My colleague Jaafar, grandson of Sayyid al-Rawi.'

"'Is that so?' she asked, interested.

"'He is in love with art, as we all are,' he added.

"'Wonderful, but does the older Rawi approve of that?' she asked.

"'It is rare that a grandfather approves of the activities of his grandson,' I replied.

"The lady turned to Muhammad Shakroun and said, 'We shall meet again soon.'

"We left feeling happy, and Muhammad Shakroun explained to me that we would soon be invited to celebrate a soirée in her house. He added, very seriously, 'She is from the al-Sadeeq family. She is the daughter of a great man and an extremely rich and cultured widow.' He fell silent for a moment, choosing his words, and then said, 'I believe she likes you.'

"I was elated. 'Are you an expert in the interpretation of women's glances?' I asked him.

"'Yes, I am. I saw her looking at you several times during the performance, even before she knew who you were.'

"'May you be right, my friend.'

"He cautioned me: 'Remember that she is a respectable woman.'

"I said, objecting, 'What a pity!'

"I thought about her. She was, undoubtedly, a precious person, and the fact that she was at least ten years my senior did not diminish her value. On the contrary, it increased her appeal. But the madness that had once ensnared me could not be repeated.

"'It is a great opportunity,' said Shakroun.

"'What do you mean?' I asked.

"'She is an excellent woman, as sweet as cream.'

"'Suppose I do not love her?' I said.

"'Is this possible? Haven't you smelled her sweet perfume?'

"I laughed loudly. Not long ago Muhammad Shakroun had fallen in love with a dancer and married her. He was happy.

※

"We went to al-Sadeeq's house in Hilmiya to celebrate the circumcision of a child. The salamlik and the garden reminded me of my grandfather's palace, though the garden was smaller and the wall was lower, and did not hide the house from the outside. A suradiq, the traditional tent, was set for us in the garden, where the fragrance of orange blossoms filled the air. It was springtime.

"Muhammad Shakroun sang with great joy, and we repeated after him with unusual enthusiasm. My voice rose above the others as I sang, 'My heart worries about you, my heart cares for you.'

"After the second part of the program, wine and drugs had a strong effect on me. I sat under an orange tree in a state of total exhaustion. When Huda Hanim came to check on us and praise our performance, I stood to greet her, swaying.

"'You are in a terrible state,' she said.

"'This is what happiness does to me,' I explained.

"She ordered that a glass of lemonade with soda be brought to me, then said, 'I like a spirit of adventure.'

"I realized she was alluding to my modest role in Muhammad Shakroun's group. I said to her, 'I decide my fate by my own free will.'

"She smiled. 'The true adventure is in man's mind.'

"'What do you mean, my lady?' I asked.

"She ignored the question and said, 'I heard exciting accounts of a misunderstanding between you and your grandfather.'

"I said, defenseless, 'So here we are. The news of my perdition is circulating among the ranks of high society.'

"She smiled charmingly and left. I felt that the gate to a new life was slowly opening. At the end of the party, Muhammad Shakroun escorted me to a café in Bab al-Khalq and talked to me in a serious tone.

"'We have to manage matters,' he said.

"I asked, mischievously, 'What matters, my skylark?'

"'Do not play dumb. I know from her lady-in-waiting that they know everything about you.'

"'Everything?'

"Shakroun went on, 'Their inquiry is meaningful.'

"'And the answers can have negative consequences,' I added.

"He stared at me inquisitively, then carried on. 'Despite everything else, you are invited to a rendezvous in the Lipton Garden. I was asked to inform you.'

"I said, shocked, 'This is beyond my imagination.'

"'It is the plain truth,' said Shakroun.

"'All right.'

"'We have to formulate a plan.'

"'You haven't asked me about my feelings for her,' I said.

"'I don't think they're hostile!'

"'Of course not.'

"'This is sufficient. I think the lady has fallen for you the way you did one day in the past,' explained Shakroun.

"'You are exaggerating,' I said.

"'Tell me, wouldn't you be happy to marry her?' he asked.

"'Do you think she has marriage in mind?'

"'She is against illegitimate relationships.'

"'Would she marry a vagabond?'

"'I know the story of a prince who left his palace to marry a vagabond,' he commented.

"I laughed.

"'What about your feelings?' he asked.

"'I admire her greatly—her personality, her beauty. Marrying her would undoubtedly make me happy.'

"'This is love, or a kind of love, or a good predisposition for love.'

"'I agree,' I said.

"'In that case, you have to take the first step, out of respect for her dignity.'

"'Provide me with more explanation, please.'

"He did, saying, 'She took the first positive steps and she is inviting you now for a romantic meeting. Would you wait like a girl for her to declare her love for you? No, you should be the one to begin out of respect for her dignity, as I already told you.'

"'Do you think so?'

"'It is a matter of good manners, first and foremost. Do not forget the sacrifices she is expected to make. Though she is free, and the wealthiest in her family, her marriage to you will lead to breakups and conflicts. I have no doubt about that. She is quite courageous to face all this.'

"'I wouldn't have believed that, had I not lived a similar experience.'

"'Exactly: you experienced a similar situation. Do not forget that she wants you, even though your ties with al-Rawi are broken and you are Marwana's previous husband and the father of four children living in Eshashal-Turguman. It is an impossibility becoming a possibility.'

"I considered the matter from all angles and was convinced, emotionally and mentally. I told Shakroun, 'If this amazing marriage takes place, I will be forced to leave my work with the band.'

"'You will certainly have to do that.'

"I wondered, 'How would I accept living with no job other than being the lady's husband?'

"He said with confidence, 'You will do something. I don't know what, but there are many jobs that require capital and human effort, and you can provide the human effort.' He added, as if to encourage me, 'Here is an adventure for you, O grand adventurer.'

"I said coldly, 'The true adventure is a response to a state of madness. This step would be taken with poise and logical thinking. It would take me from one extreme to another.'

"'To a better one,' said Shakroun.

"'So be it. I always chase the new and the exciting, armed with my usual capacity for adaptation and disregard for difficulties. Am I not living as if I have forgotten my four children? But the wound of the heart cannot heal.'

"I went to meet Huda in the Lipton Garden at the specified time. I approached her with courage and self-confidence, thus erasing our differences and making the meeting one between a man and a woman. We sat at a covered table while Umm Hussein, her lady-in-waiting, sat at a respectful distance from us. Despite her own confidence, Huda was somewhat nervous. She asked if her invitation annoyed me.

"I said boldly, 'Rest assured that it came as a fulfillment of my own dreams.'

"'Truly?' she asked.

"I went on, 'I was wishing for it to happen, but did not know how to go about it.'

"'Really? But why?'

"'This would require a long explanation. I would rather listen to you now.'

"She said eagerly, 'That is not important. Tell me why you were hoping for this meeting to take place.'

"I said in a warm voice, 'This is what a man who has fallen in love with you, with all his heart, would do.'

"She lowered her gaze, blushing, and fell into a silence that meant acceptance, happiness, and satisfaction. I repeated, 'Yes, with all my heart.'

"I recalled the situation later and did not find it embarrassing. Both my heart and my mind had accepted her. I welcomed wholeheartedly the prospect of marrying her and was not in the least interested in her fortune. Her love for me, of which I was certain, required an admission of my affection, out of consideration for her dignity. I did not lie. Or rather, I did not lie to the degree that would make me a liar. We discussed our future frankly, and I said that I had no intention of reestablishing my relationship with my grandfather, but that I doubted he would deprive me of my whole inheritance. I told her very clearly that I would be unhappy to live my life without working.

"Smiling and unperturbed, she said, 'Such concerns do not form a true obstacle to love. As for your grandfather and your inheritance, they do not matter to me. I also know that a man cannot live without work.' She added, laughing, 'But do you consider your work with the band to be a real job?'

"'It was part of a bigger adventure. That is all there is to it.'

"'I agree with you totally.'

"I thought long and hard about our love. As far as I was concerned, I had met a lady from a decent family, educated, wise, and poised, who promised a happy union. I liked her in my own way, and I rejoiced at the idea of sharing my life with her. But how could I explain her love for me? I was a lost man, an outcast, semi-employed and semi-literate, and without a future. Her love was sincere and deep, a love that did not need justification and reasoning. Her love might spring from a desire to pull me out of perdition and reshape me into a new being. If there is sadism and masochism in love, it is motivated, sometimes, by motherly feeling and a strong desire to save the other. This is how I perceived the love that bound me to Huda and led to a marriage that caused her family to sever all ties with her.

"I did not understand it then as clearly as I do now. I interpreted it in a way that satisfied my youth and my pride, and made up for the insult that I endured when Marwana abandoned me.

"I bid Muhammad Shakroun and my colleagues in the band goodbye, and took leave of the members of my religious chants band. They were all volunteers working with different second-class singers, depending on the work available. Everybody was invited to our wedding, at which Muhammad Shakroun sang. We enjoyed ourselves immensely and felt that we were bidding farewell to the age of frivolity.

"I said to Muhammad Shakroun, 'Nothing will come between us.'

"His eyes filled with tears as he replied, 'God forbid, my dearest friend.'

"The wedding was celebrated in Huda's house in Hilmiya and nobody from her family attended. The only guests were her neighbors.

"Muhammad Shakroun had hoped that my grandfather would make peace with me, with a letter, a gift, or a bouquet of flowers, but there was nothing but silence from his side. Shakroun told me that he had visited my grandfather on the occasion of the Islamic New Year. As he bent to kiss his hand, Shakroun said to him, 'It is my duty to report to you good news regarding Jaafar.'

"My grandfather ignored his words completely, which led Shakroun to add, 'He begins a new life with the honorable Huda Hanim Sadeeq.'

"My grandfather went on ignoring Shakroun's words and talked about something else that had nothing to do with me. 'Despite his attitude,' Shakroun went on to say, 'he seemed moved, and his emotion was visible in the way he held his rosary when your name was mentioned.' Shakroun advised me to take my firstborn baby to my grandfather and ask for his blessings. But I did not care about my grandfather's blessings. I was still very angry with him.

"My second honeymoon went well, filled with days of pure emotions and love. It was a time for both of us to enjoy a happy vacation before delving into an active life.

"I found myself comparing Marwana and Huda, two very different women. Marwana was a genius in the games of the body, whereas Huda raised the body to the level of the heart. Her passion was not fiery, but it provided me with a sense of security, of stability and endurance. Yet, despite this overflow of sentiment and flooding affection, I missed Marwana's eternal hell.

"So when Huda said, 'I wouldn't like you to be one more day without work,' her words couldn't have come at a better time.

"I kissed her, grateful. She added cautiously, 'Even managing my estate is not considered a convincing job, and is not an activity that would satisfy my ambition for you.'

"I asked gently, 'You have an ambition, then?'

"'Wouldn't you like to complete your studies at al-Azhar?'

"My refusal was categorical.

"'Why then did your grandfather push you in that direction?' she asked.

"'He has a special way of thinking. One day I will tell you how he views a godly human being.'

"She resumed: 'I will tell you frankly what I have in mind. I would like you to study at home.'

"'Take regular classes?' I asked.

"'Yes, until you get your high-school degree. Then I would like you to study for a higher degree, maybe specializing in law and working as a lawyer.'

"'I would need ten years,' I said.

"'Why not? Studying is in itself a kind of work. You are only twenty-five years old. This will be an advantage, making it easy for you to learn your lessons.'

"I liked the idea. 'I like studying,' I said, 'and I do not care about the years I lost. Besides, I want to work, but I do not want to be in a regular office job.'

"I began my studies with a new enthusiasm. I left the age of covert and real unemployment and entered the world of learning, which made me forget that I was a husband without work. I did not consider running Huda's estate true work, since it consisted primarily in collecting the rent, supervising some repairs and renovations, and appointing lawyers whenever needed.

"I achieved huge progress in my studies, with the occasional help of some instructors. During my free time I went with Huda to the theater and the music halls, which she loved very much. I continued drinking, despite her dislike for alcohol, but I did not get drunk, a state she despised. She made me promise to give up drugs, and whenever she saw me in Shakroun's company she reminded me of my promise. I did give them up, relying on my strong will to get me through that delicate period. Amused, Muhammad Shakroun made the following comment on my behavior: 'You can be a devil when boisterous and an angel when straight.'

"'I am determined to be somebody,' I said.

"I lived a wonderful life that reminded me of my happy days with my mother's legend and the clarity of purpose I experienced in my grandfather's house, but sometimes I was overcome with anxiety, due to my strong desire for self-accomplishment. I wanted to be somebody, but I did not know what. A knowledgeable and successful lawyer? I was enamored of the various topics I was studying and assimilated them well, with the capability of a mature person. I was attracted to them more than I had been to the religious subjects, and I learned more than was required, delving deep into various branches of knowledge. I read extensively on history, philosophy, psychology, and sociology. I was filled with a love for the truth."

※

Jaafar laughed loudly. "Imagine," he said, "the journey from the dreams of the jinn to the love of truth! What do you think?"

"It is a great journey," I said.

He went on.

"I was especially attracted to the scientific method, which contributes to the achievement of the highest degree of precision, objectivity, and integrity. Are we capable of thinking in the same way in relation to all matters in life, in order to know society, country, religion, and politics with the same precision, integrity, and objectivity?

"Huda was helping me. She was educated and had a degree from a foreign school. She had studied the foundations of science, mathematics, literature, and languages; she had studied the Arabic language with a private tutor. She was very bright and understood her lessons well. She helped me more than any teacher. She would tell me, 'A degree in itself does not matter, but it is the only acceptable way to get a job. It also gives education a more serious character.'

"She continued to help me even after her mood changed due to her pregnancy and morning sickness. We were bound together, despite our age difference and the different natures of our education. Our love grew stronger with time and was not at the mercy of whims and violent reactions.

"My life went from chaos and drug addiction to the serene life of a couple motivated by a limitless desire for knowledge. I followed a rigorous discipline that helped me shed my false semblance of freedom. It opened for me the gates of an enlightened freedom, the sort that allows a person to transcend himself through awareness, the kind of awareness that the free man appreciates, even when he perceives more powerfully the tragic nature of the unknown."

※

At that moment I interrupted Jaafar with a specific request. "Tell me about your experience with truth, freedom, and tragedy."

He laughed and asked, "Who are you talking to? You are talking to a person who does not exist anymore, a person with nothing left of him but the wasteland you see sitting with you at the Wadud Café, in al-Bab al-Akhdar. He died. I have, in fact, buried more than one personality who lived in my body, and nothing is left but this wasteland." He laughed again. "It is, nevertheless, a wasteland rich in antiquities."

He cleared his throat and said, "I loved the mind passionately, I venerated it, and that led me to the love of truth. The mind works with logic, observation, and experience to reach a pure judgment, totally free of any impediment to logic, observation, and experience. This is what I called truth.

"The mind is a relatively new creation when compared to instincts and feelings. The human being is linked to life through an instinct, and it is an instinct that connects him to existence and to the reproduction of the species. The mind plays the role of the smart servant in all that.

"Well, how can the situation be reversed? In other words, how can the mind be the first to decide and then use the instincts to serve its purpose? Can a person be convinced by a necessity, then decide to kill himself? Those who are motivated by their instincts to kill are myriad, but no one has ever killed because he was motivated by pure, sincere, and stainless thoughts. As a result, I loved the mind passionately and dreamed all the time of its absolute supremacy. I considered it the most sublime divine gift we had received. I envisioned it as the sole motivator for our existence—its sole aim, with only the mind as an inspiration for our conduct. I dreamed of a life where the mind reigned supreme, and the instincts would nestle down in obedience and submission. I wished we could erase from our culture sentences such as 'I know in my heart,' 'my feelings inspired me,' and 'the existential expression of life.'

"I concentrated my anger on the degree of consciousness and unconsciousness, and on Freud's submerged mountain, only its tip visible, since the question is not a matter of size but of value, first and foremost. I wanted the mind of the human being to be in command, to govern and control even in matters such as food and sex. What is the value of love if the mind is not totally convinced by it? Blind love would remain blind and would result, after its initial satisfaction, in nothingness, thus repeating my tragedy with Marwana. This is the reason I wanted the mind to assume its role in our intimate life the way it would in a laboratory, with the same awareness, honesty, and objectivity. We should, as a result, change our songs, our yearnings, and our dreams.

"I don't pretend to have attained this high level. It is even possible that my inability to do so was an important factor in my tragedy. I do not preach the disregard of instincts or the underrating of them, but I long to avoid their negative impact on the truth. Imagine us free of submission to ego, capable of evaluating our countries without the influence of what we call patriotism. Generally speaking, the wise human being became my goal, as the godly human being had been in the past."

I said to Jaafar, "Some writers have painted a frightening picture of this logical concept of the world."

"I know that. It is because they approached it with sick, romantic, stupid hearts. But I believe that the mind will one day help the human being do without his instincts and emotions, and they will all become as useless as the body's appendix."

"But how did your life turn upside-down so tragically?" I asked.

"I told you before that I proceed in life by impulsive leaps. I discovered the world of the mind suddenly and it fascinated me. I became aware that I had been experimenting in the void, and I was now invited to venture truly into the world of the mind. That was the genuine adventure."

"What about freedom?" I asked with interest.

"Freedom is like an adventure. You practice it sometimes, for the enjoyment of the instincts, the way I enjoyed Marwana, wine, and narcotics. But that is slavery masquerading as freedom. True freedom, on the other hand, is an awareness of the mind, its message, and its objectives. It consists in determining freely the means to be used, and organizing them meticulously in a manner that causes them to act like chains. It is therefore freedom masquerading as slavery. This is how my life proceeded in the house in Manyal. There was a time for studies, a time for free reading, and a time for discussions, promenades, and love. It traveled on a long road over which I raised the flag of reason."

Interrupting, I asked him to tell me about the tragedy.

He sighed and said, "Be patient. It was a private tragedy. First I want to submit to you my vision of a public tragedy, that of the wise human being. Before the creation of the mind, man was in harmony with himself and his life: a life of harsh struggle. He did not seem to have a choice but to endure it, like any other animal. When he received the gift of the mind and began creating civilization, he bore a new charge, an inevitable responsibility, and one that he was not qualified to assume. It was then that he became aware of the full view, that his life on earth was the life of a single being, despite the obvious contradictions. The truth of the matter is that that man was and continues to be in a period of transition where the instincts and the mind are both present. The instincts oppose whatever the mind advises, and to this day, the instincts always win—at least in public life.

"The mind achieved total supremacy only in the sciences. Apart from that, it submits to the instincts, and even the achievements of science are gobbled up by the instincts. Though the mind maintains its own language in the field of research, the language that appeals to the masses continues to be the language of emotions and instincts, as evidenced by songs about sex, the homeland, racial discrimination, stupid dreams, and blunders. This is the public tragedy, and its red clouds won't vanish until the voice of reason rises and instincts wither and cease to exist.

"My personal tragedy, however, was the result of the struggle between my mind and my unshakable belief in God. I was faced with the question that begged to be asked: how could I maintain my faith if I wanted to make the mind my guide and my inspiration? Consequently, my trust in pure faith was shaken, and so was my belief in the language of the heart. It was up to the mind to resolve this dilemma with its own strength. To deny that the mind was not created for this purpose is nothing short of an admission of failure, and to suggest replacing it with the heart or with spontaneity is another admission of failure."

※

"What did your mind tell you to do?" I asked.

"My mind failed completely to comprehend God, or even envision Him, but it could not help but assume His presence. This is the tragedy, because if people believe that the problem is artificial and it is possible to live without thinking about it, everything loses its meaning, no matter how much meaning we attribute to all things with the power of our imagination, will, and courage. I envy those who live happily and die contented, having not known a god.

"I shared my worries with Huda, who has an unwavering faith, so strong that she never neglected a prayer or a day of fasting.

"She told me, 'It is impossible to accept the universe without the existence of God. Don't you see the continuous acts of creation taking place under our own eyes, in the world of plants, animals, and human beings? It is not possible to doubt the power of creation.'

"'I want a very close connection and a strong conviction, like one plus one equals two,' I said.

"'We are talking about the heart as the source of faith,' she replied. 'But remember that only the man who reasons believes in God. Reason is in fact the foundation of faith, but man's relative inability to be sentient, despite his aspirations to it, makes him assign faith to another organ of the body, to avoid contradiction.'

"'The human being became aware of life, death, and fear,' I said, 'and so he ordered his mind to safeguard hope. Even Moses himself wanted to see God.'"

✳

At this point I asked him, "What about your faith now, Jaafar?"

He threw his head back, and with his weak eyes looked at the stream of stars between the minaret of al-Hussein Mosque on the one side and the old houses on the other. "I am unable to deny God's existence!" he whispered.

✳

He went on narrating his story. "I progressed in my studies and achieved huge success. I became more aware and acquired a diverse culture. I had four boys. It was the happiest and the most fulfilling period in my life.

"Muhammad Shakroun was in charge of the legal alimony to Marwana. When my oldest son reached the legal age to live with me, I decided to use my right to claim him. Huda did not object when I informed her of my decision, but I found out that Marwana had remarried and gone with her husband and the children to live in an oasis. Some said she went to Libya. I was extremely sad.

"My friendship with Shakroun remained intact. We prayed each Friday in al-Hussein Mosque, then ate lunch in Hilmiya. Shakroun's Islam was limited to the Friday prayer and abstaining from alcohol during the month of Ramadan. He explained to me that artists like him would be judged more leniently, due to their life conditions and the needs of their profession. His success as a second-class singer was established. His popular songs became known and were available on records. He moved with his family to Rod al-Farag, but he never had children.

"He remained my only friend until I met colleagues from Khan Jaafar, who were ahead of me in their studies and worked as lawyers and teachers. I benefited from them, but that was not their only impact on my life, as you will see.

"My children were my main source of happiness. They were extremely handsome and healthy. The oldest was a copy of his great-grandfather, al-Rawi.

"I heard very little about my grandfather, only what Shakroun reported to me. As he grew older, he kept to his house, leaving it only for the Friday prayer at the mosque. He limited the number of receptions for his friends. Those who frequented his home had the impression that with age he had forgotten his past and present preoccupations. I wondered whether I would be more than a memory in his heart.

"I continued my studies and obtained my law degree. Huda generously provided me with a law office in Bab al-Khalq, and furnished it with a valuable library and fine furniture, the kind that is found in the offices of famous lawyers.

"Thus began a new phase in my life."

7

The office attorney was at the center of activities. He was in charge of minor cases that were quite suitable for a young lawyer at the beginning of his career. I was, in fact, his assistant, and my work revolved around his activities. But my office became the meeting place for my friends, especially those whose opinion I sought while studying law. They were originally distant travel companions, but throughout our regular meetings they achieved the political conquest of my soul.

"I want you to know that I was not totally disconnected from politics, as you might think. Among the numerous guests in my grandfather's house, I met those who shared the same ideas as these new companions. They praised the elite, who, in their view, must rule for the benefit of the elite, for the masses, and for the homeland. The discussion often revolved around the charter, not as a base for a government of the people, but as a document that validated the elite's rule and confirmed them vis-à-vis the ruler. It was as if the field of government was available only for the ruler and the elite.

"I admired their grandiose looks, their thick mustaches, and their tidy beards. They would debate quietly, and spoke extensively about knowledge and education, about study missions and the renewal of religious thinking. They never made a secret of their disdain for the riffraff and their rule. They insisted on the necessity of a long-term education for the people, and a continuous awareness that would allow them a modest participation in political life.

"One evening, I heard my grandfather ask them, 'Politics in your opinion is therefore like Sufism, inaccessible to outsiders?'

"They answered in the affirmative, which made my grandfather wonder, 'Who would look after the interests of the commoners?'

"'We are the owners of the agencies that matter,' they replied. 'We are the masters of agriculture, trade, and industry. As for the masses, they do not need more than a craft to earn a living, and some services.'

"I was convinced by that theory, and accepted it as the best means to run matters in an orderly fashion. I thanked God for being a member of the elite and not the masses.

"Exciting times arrived then, as the voice of the people rose high and filled the space. The masses demonstrated in large numbers, pouring in like a flood. I watched them from the roof of my grandfather's palace, surprised and happy.

"Despite all that, I was never drawn to the political realm. I was convinced that I could experience life, its good and its bad, without ever getting involved in politics.

"I became, unexpectedly, strongly involved in politics for the first time, in my office in Bab al-Khalq. I struggled with the concepts of liberalism, socialism, communism, anarchism, the Salafiya movement, and fascism. I found myself in a raging whirlwind that made my head spin. Following my belief in the holiness of the mind, I turned to it for guidance in the midst of that turmoil.

"One day I was reviewing various ideologies with Professor Saad Kabir. His is the only name I will mention, because of the dangerous role he played in my life, while the others had a minimal impact on me.

"'What are you?' he asked me.

"'Nothing,' I said hesitantly.

"'It is death,' he said, furious. He was a very sensitive man, and extremely nervous, despite his intelligence and vast knowledge. I objected, saying, 'But I am a diligent student who worships the mind.'

"'Can the mind fulfill its purpose without providing an opinion on the system of human rule?'

"'But . . . but politics serve specific interests,' I said.

"'Interests guide the average person to his political party, but a bright mind is able to discriminate between good and evil,' he explained.

"Smiling, I asked, 'In your opinion, in what direction are my interests guiding me?'

"'With the mind you should be able to go beyond your position,' he replied.

"'I have to give myself more time for reflection,' I said.

"I shared my concerns with Huda, since she was my best friend. I had no secrets from her. She said without hesitation, 'I've noticed that politics is destructive to the mind.'

"My answer reflected my inner struggle, as I said to her, 'This depends on the mind itself.'

"She spoke with conviction: 'In politics, the mind finds itself in an ordeal.'

"'Maybe,' I said. 'But running away from it is not the solution.'

"I must admit that thinking had become an intrinsic part of my life, and I was strongly challenged by what I had heard in my office. I started wondering about the significance of all that. Despite the reciprocal and sincere feelings of friendship between my friends and me, I had no doubt that some of them regarded my higher social class with true dislike. As a result, I began for the first time to consider this situation as the source of a socio-political struggle. It was as if I had awakened to find myself lying over the mouth of a volcano.

"As the grandson of al-Rawi, I belonged to the feudalistic class. This put my interests in agreement with the rule of the elite, and might not differ sharply from the religious Salafi ideology. But I did not agree with popular liberalism. As for the communists and the socialists, they were my natural enemies—it was like the enmity between cat and mouse. This was my thinking, but I wondered if I would be able to use the mind to assess those different sects in all honesty. Or would I be betrayed by emotions and use the mind as a clever slave? I could seek peace by avoiding politics, but I believed that this position was not in any way compatible with the respect and veneration of the mind. Politics was life.

"My dialogue with Saad Kabir continued as I found in his position the true challenge, a forceful confrontation. I told him once, 'Politics is a vast world whose charms are distributed between all ideologies!'

"His dark face and small features became stiff. 'You are forgiven your hesitation, because an idea needs an incubation period.'

"'Be patient with me,' I said. 'I find the elite noble, cultured, and possessed of a historical authenticity.'

"'It is possible, in a fair social system, for everyone to rise to the level of the elite,' he said.

"I thought about that, then said, 'There are freedom, values, and human rights of great beauty in liberalism.'

"'This was all used to serve the interests of a special social class,' he said.

"I said, with the same sincerity, 'There is in communism full justice that provides human ideologies with the possibility to open up and thrive.'

"'That is probably the least that can be said about it.'

"I continued, 'And in religion there are countless balanced benefits.'

"He lost his temper. 'Damn it!' he said.

71

"Disregarding his anger, I said, 'We seek the truth no matter how long we fumble.'

"Huda was an authentic libertarian and considered the British system ideal. She was following my reflections with concerned interest. I asked her one day, 'Why are you worried, Huda?'

"'Thinking about politics,' she said sincerely, 'might be followed by political activities, and it is a matter not devoid of danger.'

"I took a deep breath. 'Safety is a beautiful thing, but there are in life things more important than safety.'

"'This is why I sometimes feel that my happy household is facing a threat,' she said.

"I kissed her and said, 'Be courageous, as I have always known you to be.'

"'It is fashionable nowadays for young people to believe in communism,' she told me.

"'I only think, my darling, and I am not concerned by what is fashionable in any way whatsoever.'

"And so I went on studying and thinking."

✳

At this point Jaafar laughed so loudly that his voice disturbed both those sleeping and those roving this historical district.

"What is so funny?" I asked.

"I will tell you a secret I never shared with anybody, not even with my friendly wife," he replied.

"Truly?"

"It once occurred to me that there were some similarities between my life and that of the Prophet!"

He paused, but when I did not comment, he carried on. "My father died when I was quite young and my mother died when I was hardly five. It was my grandfather who raised me. I viewed my departure from my grandfather's house as a kind of emigration."

"But the Prophet did not emigrate for the sake of adventure," I said.

72

"Of course not, of course not. It is merely a resemblance, not a conformity between the two lives. There was my marriage to an honorable upper-class woman who was older than me. She provided me with opportunities to study and reflect. I considered all that, but then it occurred to me that I was also a man with a mission."

"A religious mission?" I asked, laughing.

"Let's say a mission of a new kind. I was fascinated by the idea, and it quickly enthralled me. I pursued my studies and reflection, and continuously reminded myself of the tricks of instincts and emotions in order to purify my thinking and keep it unblemished.

"My first conclusion was related to our social order, which I found to be illogical, unjust, and responsible for all our ills: our poverty, illiteracy, and sickness. I also concluded that I was not a member of the elite as I had often thought, but a member of a gang. Huda objected to this description and alluded to her ancestors' honorable origins. I analyzed the sources of wealth—gifts, opportunism, exploitation, oppression, and force—until I was convinced that there was no legal wealth in the strict meaning of the word.

"Saad Kabir encouraged me: 'This is a good direction and promises a happy ending, but you have to start with argumentative materialism and historical materialism.'

"I told him with confidence, 'I have the same position regarding all philosophies, and Marxist philosophy is only one of many philosophies. Why does it have to turn into a creed, and why does it impose itself by force and dictatorship?'

"'It is not a philosophy. It was revealed through the heaven of theoretical reflection, to be applied to people's lives. Let's give humanity hope. It deserves to be an article of faith.'

"I said, reluctantly, 'To make an authoritative assertion in favor of materialism is not more powerful, in the realm of the mind, than confirming authoritatively the existence of God.'

"'You are still an idealist.'

"I shouted, 'Do not throw strange accusations at me. Stay within the limits of an objective discussion.'

73

"He calmed down and advised me to study. 'You need more lessons,' he said.

"'But I am not convinced by that theory, while I consider social justice to be obvious without the need for a theory.'

"I devoted more time to my studies. My heart became an arena for a hellish struggle. During this period I spent little time with my wife and rarely played with my children. I was overcome with the idea of a mission as a promising and powerful force, albeit a modest mission, because I vowed to save humanity only in Egypt. I was constantly thinking and rethinking, warning myself repeatedly lest my thinking slide down the slippery roads of emotions and inherited beliefs. Finally I decided to write down my thoughts to ensure clarity in my thinking."

I asked Jaafar if he had done so.

"Yes," he said.

"Did you publish them in a book?"

"No, my circumstances did not make it possible."

"Do you remember their content?" I asked.

He laughed, and quickly summarized his thoughts: "I presented a concise survey of the history of political and social movements, from feudalism to communism. Then I described my project based on three tenets: a philosophical principle, a social doctrine, and a system of government. The adoption of a philosophical principle is left to the interested person to choose, whether it is materialism, spiritualism, or even Sufism. The social doctrine is communist in its essence. It is based on collective ownership, the abolishment of private property and inheritance, total equality, and the elimination of all forms of exploitation. It is guided by the following motto: 'From each according to his ability, to each according to his need.' As for the system of government, it is democratic, based on the multi-party system, the separation of power, and the protection of all sorts of freedom—except free ownership—and human values. One can generally say that my system is the logical heir of Islam, the French Revolution, and the communist revolution.

"I gave a copy of the manuscript to Saad Kabir and told him that it contained my opinion. He was surprised and couldn't believe I'd written it.

"I told him, 'Your famous characterizations, such as bourgeois, conciliatory, and unifier, won't deter me. I have the right to formulate a new doctrine if I am not convinced by the existing ones.'

"He became suspicious and said carefully, 'On condition that you create a real new doctrine and not concoct one out of existing doctrines.'

"'All doctrines are subject to a give-and-take process,' I said angrily.

"Saad Kabir read the manuscript in my office in a little over two hours. When he finished, he took a deep breath and muttered, 'It is no use.'

"I was waiting eagerly for his opinion. He muttered again, as if talking to himself, 'It is a mixture of fish, milk, and tamarind.'

"'Explain!' I said.

"He spoke nervously. 'Concocted daydreams, imagination, an assemblage of discordant ideas. It is nothing.'

"'Is this your final opinion?' I asked.

"'What did you expect?'

"'I expected you to be convinced by what I wrote.'

"'And then?'

"'Then we can form an association, an organization, or a party,' I explained.

"He laughed coldly. 'What a pity!'

"I said, angry again, 'You all are devoid of a free will and the capacity to think!'

"He replied, adopting a very serious tone, 'You at least know that my colleagues and I are serious; that we risk our lives and believe in the human being.'

"'I believe in the human being more than you do," I said, 'and I do not believe that a true believer in the human being can accept a dictatorial regime. I, too, am serious, and am willing to risk my life.'

"'What are you planning to do?' he asked.

"'I want to form an association or a political party.'

"'When he got up to leave, he said sternly, 'We will come back to this, again and again.'

"Before I called for the formation of an association, I consulted with my wife. She was extremely disturbed, having read the manuscript

75

carefully. She told me, 'You are a man of law and you know that the constitution of this country considers communism a crime.'

"'Communism is one thing and my doctrine is something else.'

"'You are calling for a communist social order, and this is what matters for the law and those who wrote it.'

"'I can change the phrasing of the second clause. I find the word socialism acceptable, and though I believe in God, I do not want to impose religion on anyone. Furthermore, I am attached to the democratic system as it is applied in the West. Won't all that protect me from suspicion?'

"'I do not think so, my darling,' she said. 'I see you truly as a pure communist in the fundamental matter, which concerns the haves and the have-nots.'

"'The problem, Huda, is that you do not believe in me.'

"'I believe in democracy,' she said, 'and I consider the democratic system missing only the humane protection of the masses in order to reach perfection. I have no doubt that an English citizen, for example, has a better life than a Russian citizen.'

"'I do not share that belief,' I said.

"She replied, somewhat despondent, 'Well, we have agreed on everything up till now; I suppose it is time for us to disagree!'

"Meanwhile, Saad Kabir was trying to convince Huda to adopt Marxism.

"Huda and I often invited our friends to dinner at our house. I invited Muhammad Shakroun to join us, but he did not appreciate their company and found their discussions boring.

"You should probably know more about Saad Kabir. He was among the friends who came to my office for discussions. They represented all doctrines, even the feudal system of the past, but Saad Kabir was most concerned about my fate. He was a proselytizing lawyer, well versed in his field, extremely cultured, and greatly appreciated in debates and lectures. He was irascible by nature, tenacious, clinging obdurately to his beliefs. He was one of those single-minded people who never hesitated to destroy his enemy by any means, whether through rhetorical skills or illogical arguments. His destructive tendencies upset those, like myself, who respected the mind and worshiped it.

"I noticed in Huda's eyes a certain admiration for him. She easily gave in to his forceful and enthusiastic arguments.

"One day, Muhammad Shakroun told me that he did not like my friends.

"'They are kind,' I said.

"'Maybe,' he replied, 'but the man called Saad Kabir is not kind.'

"'But he is an excellent man in every sense of the word.'

"'Maybe, but he is more clever than necessary.'

"I laughed and agreed with him, but he went on, saying, 'Do not open your door to just anybody.'

"I felt in his words a kind of warning. Curious, I asked him what he meant.

"He tried to dodge the question, saying, 'I simply do not trust him.'

"'Explain,' I said vehemently.

"'He is the conceited type and is not worthy of your trust.'

"'You mean more than what you are saying.'

"'Not at all, and I swear by the head of al-Hussein!'

"After this conversation, I could not go back to my previous trust of Saad Kabir, and started observing what was going on around me, carefully and suspiciously. My dignity did not permit me, however, to change the order of things. Had I done so, I would have upset Huda, a decent lady, and I would have lost her respect. But I continued watching Saad Kabir when he was at our home, consumed by anxiety and vigilance. He would get absorbed in his discussions with Huda, and she with him. I noticed that she liked his rhetorical style. It invigorated her, and she seemed always eager for more. At the end of one of those evenings, I said to her, 'I won't be surprised if you suddenly tell me that you are a communist.'

"She asked, smiling, 'Were you fooled by my interest in his conversation?'

"'And the way you were moved by it,' I said.

"'He is an excellent man,' she replied. 'That is why I feel sorry for him.'

"Huda was in her early fifties at that time, and Saad Kabir was in his thirties. Though I had nothing left in my heart for Huda but a deep friendship, I worried. I wondered what Shakroun had meant, if he had noticed more than I did, and if he hid anything from me. Was Huda going through a midlife crisis? But she had always been a model of wisdom and poise, and continued to be. I could not find any reason to suspect Saad Kabir. Not a glance, a gesture, or a word. Despite all that, my sacred mind was shaken, and I fell victim to mysterious, brooding emotions.

"Then the tragedy hit me like an earthquake, without any warning."

❋

Jaafar fell into total silence.

I repeated, "A tragedy?"

He laughed, but did not utter a word. I asked again, "A tragedy? What did you say?"

"The tragedy occurred as I was getting ready to form my political party," he replied.

"What happened?"

He sighed, then explained: "I was getting ready to embark on a battle, to defy the left and the right. I was alone in my office with Saad Kabir. Our conversation was heated, a normal thing for him but unusual for me. He said, 'You think that you are the author of a metaphysical social political doctrine, but any doctrine would require a whole life to formulate. The reader, on the other hand, gleans all the different doctrines during a year or two, and might consider participating in an election that he believes to be an exercise in rational thought, whereas it is merely a process to combine all the contradictory doctrines that people can conceive. This would provide us with as many doctrines as there are literate people in the world.'

"'Insolent, rude!' I shouted.

"He looked at me in shock. 'What?'

"I repeated, 'Insolent, rude.'

78

"'Have you forgotten that you are talking to your teacher?' he said angrily.

"I jumped at him and slapped him, and he slapped me back. We engaged in a frightening fight, and there was no one to separate us. I was stronger than he but he was younger than me, and when I started gasping, I grabbed the letter opener."

Jaafar was silent for a long time. When he spoke again, I tried to imagine the scene as he described it: "I can't forget his face. I mean, after I dug the sharp letter opener into his neck. His face slowly lost its life and fell into the depths of darkness. He stopped fighting back and submitted to the unknown, leaving behind his debates, his bright mind and glory. Everything came to an end."

"You killed a man, Jaafar!" I shouted.

"Yes, Jaafar al-Rawi had become a killer."

"What a pity!" I said.

Jaafar went on describing the crime scene: "I stood there, looking at his body lying between the desk and the leather sofa, in a state of eternal icy dazedness. I felt as if I had unloaded in one move all of life's burdens and emotions. Then I plunged, suddenly, into the depths of the world of knowledge; and I saw through a crack in its crumbling wall the phantom of the tragedy running away from me, running to a different and opposite universe with which I had no human contact. Then I heard a voice, maybe my own voice or maybe someone else's, shouting, 'Oh my blessed mind, why have you abandoned me?'"

"What a pity," I said again.

"From the head of a party to a life sentence."

After a short but intense silence, I asked him, "Was there an excuse for the murder?"

"On the one hand, there is always a justification for killing; but on the other hand, nothing justifies a murder."

79

I rephrased my question. "I mean, did you find anything to confirm your suspicions about your wife and therefore justify the murder?"

"Believe me, there was nothing at all. My wife's breakdown over her concern for me confirmed my stupidity. It was as if the tragedy had occurred to ridicule the worshiper of the mind, that was all."

"Was there any mention of your suspicions during the trial?" I asked.

"No, and I categorically refused that approach. The case was presented as a struggle between two communists that led to murder. In prison, I insisted on the status of a political criminal, but they considered me plainly and simply a killer. To this day I consider myself a political criminal. What do you think?"

"You are probably a semi-political criminal," I said.

"But if it were not for politics, the crime would not have occurred."

"Maybe. But what was your grandfather's reaction?" I asked.

"A few days before the accident, Muhammad Shakroun informed me that my grandfather was very ill, and suggested I visit him together with Huda and my children. I discussed the matter with Huda and she welcomed the idea. We postponed the visit to Friday, but the crime occurred on Thursday evening, and I never received a word from him. I do not even know if he learned of my crime.

"Though I requested to be treated like a political criminal in prison, there is no difference between the treatment of the political criminal and of the regular criminal. My request made me the subject of ridicule and jokes, and I was punished with lashes for causing commotion. Huda visited me only once."

"Why did she stop after that?"

"She passed away," he said.

He continued telling me his story: "I was very sad and I worried about the children. But Muhammad Shakroun told me that the children's maternal aunt had offered to care for them and had taken them to Minya to live with her. I have no doubt that they forgot me very quickly, as I had forgotten my mother. In a second visit, Shakroun told me that he was going on a tour in North Africa, and that was the last I heard from him. Jaafar al-Rawi died, and so did the world outside the walls of the prison.

"I promoted my new doctrine in prison, but was faced with ignorance, passivity, and sarcasm. I even extended an invitation to join my party to the prison warden, who was kind to me because of my family background, my profession, and my bad luck.

"My eyesight weakened in prison, and I contracted many illnesses. I left in the condition you see me in today."

8

I am in shambles, an old sick man, half blind, with a handful of memories that no one can believe, but I have not lost my clarity of mind or my strong determination, and the seduction of debates is still alive in my heart.

"I thought that if I found Muhammad Shakroun, I would be able to locate the link that would take me to the heart of matters. But there was no trace of him, and I did not meet anyone who knew him, as if he had not entertained a generation of Egyptians with his voice. At the Institute of Oriental Music I was told that Shakroun lived for some time in Morocco, but that since then no one had heard from him.

"I went to the Hilmiya Palace and found a huge building in its place, property of an insurance company. I had inherited a large sum of money from my wife, but spent most of it in prison on cigarettes and other matters, and I had hardly any money left. I went to Eshashal-Turguman but found no trace of the old place. It had become a modern suburb with a park and a gas station.

"I met many of my old colleagues, some retired, others still working in the field of law. I must tell you, though, that no one tried to avoid me. On the contrary, some received me very warmly. There were those who had kept their enthusiasm for their own doctrines, while others had been pulled away by life's worries and its needs.

"I wondered where Marwana's and Huda's children were! But I decided that no good would come of finding them and that I had better leave them alone.

"I find pleasure sometimes in imagining their lives and those of their children—my grandchildren. There are certainly among them bandits and judges, and they are possibly more numerous than I think. I might meet them in my wanderings, but I wouldn't recognize them and they wouldn't recognize me.

"Once all those pressing matters were settled, I thought about resuming my struggle for my doctrine and establishing my party. But I faced insurmountable obstacles, among them my advanced age, my extreme frailty, and my appearance, which provoked pity and sometimes disgust. A leader, as you well know, must have a charismatic and appealing personality. Furthermore, the field of politics was filled with lively and influential people. I told myself that I had better write down my theory in a book. If I failed to do so, however—which was a distinct possibility—I would still preach my doctrine wherever I went. It might be picked up by someone more capable than I; someone who would make it work.

"I was convinced then that all I had left to do was face a forced short rest, before the eternal rest."

✺

Jaafar fell silent for quite a long time, then whispered calmly, "Al-Rawi's face came back to me from my past memory."

As I was about to speak, he continued. "I did not doubt that he had died, but I wondered about his money and his palace. I stood under the walls of the huge palace, as imposing as a mountain, then slipped toward the blind alley, toward the gate. To my surprise it was ajar."

Jaafar stopped for a few seconds, then went on, "I pushed the gate and went in. I was surprised by what I saw. I had never expected or imagined it would happen. There was no garden and no salamlik. The flowers and their scent were gone, and so was the chirping of the birds.

There was nothing left but a huge wasteland with piles of garbage and a group of beggars."

I shouted in my surprise: "What happened? Was it demolished?"

"There was nothing but waste everywhere, surrounded by the high walls and the imposing front gate. The beggars looked at me with concern and fear, but I stomped my feet on the ground and went to see if any of my grandfather's companions were still alive. I learned that al-Rawi had died one year after my imprisonment, and that he had spent all his wealth on charitable organizations and the needy, without leaving me or any of my descendants a single penny. As for the palace, it had been destroyed when a bomb fell on it during one of the aerial attacks on Cairo, and the rubble had been cleared out. This is the whole story from beginning to end. I soon realized that I wouldn't get any peace during the short period of respite that precedes the eternal rest. I also decided to set up house in the ruins of my grandfather's palace. There I sleep, usually between dawn and forenoon, like any beggar."

He laughed a short laugh. I said with pity, "An unhappy old age."

"No!" he shouted. "I refuse pity and compassion. Never forget that you are talking to a great man, and a proof of his greatness is his ability to adapt to the most difficult of conditions and situations, and face them with pride and a smile!"

I was convinced, and said, "Anyhow, the monthly financial support which—"

He interrupted me sharply. "I have made a decision regarding that!"

"I don't think you are serious about your decision."

"I am extremely serious," he retorted.

"Do you mean that you won't write the petition?"

"I certainly won't!"

"This is pure madness," I said.

"Call it whatever you like. Since al-Rawi deprived me of my inheritance, I refuse to beg for even one penny of it!"

"Jaafar, you are old, weak, and poor, and the little money you have left will soon be spent."

"I know all that very, very well, but I am more stubborn than al-Rawi himself."

"Let me write the petition."

"I refuse," he said.

I protested, but he insisted, saying, "I will not discuss the subject anymore."

There was silence. He was a tired storyteller and I was a tired listener. I yawned.

He laughed and said, "I do not yawn before dawn."

I mumbled listlessly, "Bravo."

"I am a roaming beggar. I leave al-Rawi's wasteland to wander in the streets, from Margush to al-Khurunfish to al-Nahhasin and finally to Khan Jaafar. Everywhere I go I have a memory and a secret. There are memories in al-Hilmiya, and in Bab al-Khalq Square my heart beats. Everywhere I go I spread my doctrine. I invite humanity to save itself."

"Your doctrine?" I inquired.

"Yes."

"You do that openly?"

"Yes."

"You must be wary of troubles," I warned.

"I do not fear troubles."

I told myself that his appearance did not convey seriousness and he was not in any danger.

We both fell silent, nearly lulled into an exhausted sleep.

In that moment of inertia and sorrow, we heard the voice of the muezzin floating over the waves of obscurity. Jaafar stretched and said in his harsh voice, "It is time for us to go."

We walked side by side on our way to the square.

Jaafar whispered, "Let life be filled with holy madness to the last breath."

My head was ringing with the talk of the night.

Glossary

Alamiya: diploma awarded by al-Azhar in Egypt at the end of the specified period of study.

awalim: traditional women singers.

fuul: cooked fava beans, usually eaten for breakfast.

gallabiya: long loose garment worn by men in Egypt.

gibba: long garment worn under the *quftan* by imams and students enrolled in al-Azhar, preparing them to assume the responsibility of imam.

kawari: a dish consisting of sheep trotters.

Laylat al-Qadr: the night that falls between the 26th and the 27th of Ramadan. It marks the night on which the Quran was revealed.

mahmal: the litter once sent to Mecca by the Egyptian government during the Hajj (pilgrimage) carrying the covering for the Kaaba. The name is derived from the verb *hamala*, 'to carry.'

quftan: long outer coat worn by imams over the gibba.

Salafi: follower of a reform movement in Islam launched by Muhammad Abduh in Egypt.

salamlik: word of Turkish origin referring to a reception room.

Samadiya: derived from al-Samad, one of God's attributes and meaning 'the master obeyed by all.' The Samadiya is the chapter in the Quran entitled 'Surat al-Ikhlas.'

85

suradiq: a large tent erected to receive a large number of guests outside the house for either happy events or a death in the family.

tawashih: a form of Arabic poetry consisting of stanzas, often set to music and sung.

tuzz: expression used to mean 'so what! I couldn't care less.'

waqf: plural *awqaf*, consists in endowing private property for charitable purposes. The income generated by *awqaf* or the services they provide (hospitals, schools, libraries) are aimed at the needy. In Egypt, where this novel takes place, *awqaf* are run by the Ministry of Awqaf, a government agency. The concept of the waqf dates back to the time of the Prophet Muhammad and has undergone transformations throughout history. The waqf par excellence is the Kaaba in Mecca.